D0455170

Hit

Other novels by Lorie Ann Grover

Firstborn: A Novel
Hold Me Tight
On Pointe
Loose Threads

Hit

inspired by a true story

LORIE ANN GROVER

BLINK

BLINK

Hit
Copyright © 2014 by Lorie Ann Grover

This title is also available as a Blink ebook.
Visit www.zondervan.com/ebooks.

Requests for information should be addressed to:

Blink, 3900 Sparks Drive SE, *Grand Rapids, Michigan 49546*

ISBN 978-0-310-72950-1

Song of Solomon quote on page 151 is taken from the American Standard Version of
the Bible.

Cover design: Brand Navigation
Cover photo: Masterfile Corporation, iStockphoto LP/Prill Mediendesign & Fotographie
Interior composition: Greg Johnson, Textbook Perfect

Printed in the United States of America

14 15 16 17 18 19 /DCI/ 22 21 20 19 18 17 16 15 14 13 12 11 10 9 8 7 6 5 4 3 2 1

*Dedicated to the McCormicks, especially Sarah,
who lived through their trial with so much more grace
than my characters do.
With my love to you each.*

*And great thanks and appreciation
to Elizabeth Harding, Jacque Alberta, Emma Dryden,
and David Hammermaster.*

Tell Me

by Langston Hughes

Why should it be my loneliness,
Why should it be my song,
Why should it be my dream
deferred
overlong?

PART 1

Day One

CHAPTER 1

Sarah

6:54 am

In our pristine, beige kitchen, I slap my palm on the cover of the Mills College catalog. Pieces of sky still shine brightly between my fingers. I shove the booklet under the pile of bills Dad sets down.

"I wish you'd put the mail where it belongs, Mark," says Mom.

Choosing a cereal bowl, he doesn't answer. She sighs and nudges her way around him to the granite counter and slots each envelope into the stand inside the glass-paned cupboard.

"And let's put this right here." She props the Mills catalog in her cookbook stand.

"Really, Mom?" I protest.

"What?" she asks, all innocent, and I refuse to answer. The

catalog's on full display, awash in a heavenly glow from the recessed light above; one more effort to wear me down.

Mom picks up her phone from the charger. "No riding the bus this morning, Sarah," she says, disappearing down the carpeted hall.

"I'm taking the bus," I mutter.

Out the dark, rain-tapped window, a crow caws fiercely, but leaning forward, I can't spot the threat. The February chill rustles the empty birch branches, making them scrabble like worried, bony fingers. Our Space Needle-shaped thermometer says it's forty-five degrees out there. Not too bad.

In the reflection, I smooth my eyebrow, then push my poem for Mr. Haddings deeper inside the back pocket of my jeans. As far as I can jam it.

"Mom, it's not like riding the bus is going to kill me." I tug my messenger bag on. Reaching around my dad, I stash the Cheerios in the lower cupboard and brush past the Mills scholarship letter Mom hung on the fridge. I turn back and stick the University of Washington magnet right smack in the middle of the paper. "Heading to the bus stop," I call out to Mom.

She peeks into the kitchen, her mascara wand balanced in her fingertips. "But, Sarah, it's raining, and you already have that postnasal drip." She heads to the bathroom, raising her voice. "I know you like to ride in with Cydni, but you need to take care of yourself, first and foremost. That said, there's no time for me to take you with the early estate showing I have this morning. It's that property on the edge of town I was telling you about. Anyway, it means you'll have to ride in with Luke."

"But Cydni needs to look over my homework on the bus, and Luke will get me there too late for some stuff I have to do."

At the kitchen island, my brother scoots the stool closer and looks up from his Chex, a milk droplet suspended on his lower lip. "Yeah, I'm not near ready to go," he answers. "Go ahead and ride the bus, Sares, even though it's totally lame for seniors."

I sneer at him.

"Even as a junior, I wouldn't. Because"—he wipes his lip on his sleeve—"I bought my own truck."

"Yeah, well, your truck is lame."

"Is not. It's a decent truck, you moron."

"Luke, don't call your sister a moron," Mom calls out.

He huffs. "Why don't you buy your own car, Sares?"

"Because I'm saving for tuition," I retort.

"And ignoring the free ride to that all-girl's school," he sing-songs. "Right, Mom?"

"I'm going to UW and won't need a car on campus," I explain for the thousandth time.

"Mills is the better choice for you, Sarah!" Mom pipes in.

I throw my head back and close my eyes. Breathe.

Luke gets up and leaves his bowl behind. Loping past me, he leans close and smiles. "I'm not taking you, Sares, 'cause I don't like to advertise that we're related."

I go to smack him on the back of his head, but he ducks. Leaving the kitchen, he laughs and thumps down the split-level stairs to his room.

"Sarah …" Mom nags.

I step into the hall, tugging my hair out from under the strap of my bag.

Mom rushes past me into the living room, checking a text. "Sarah, you are beautiful no matter what you wear, but the new

11

blue shirt I picked up for you really fits better than that one you have on under your hoodie, sweetie."

Ugh! Did I ask her?

Straightening the issues of *Elle* and *Golf Digest* on the coffee table, she calls to Dad. "Mark, can you drive her?"

Still at the kitchen counter, he's peeling his daily banana and reading from his Bible. "Mark?"

No answer. *For once, thanks for being checked out, Dad.*

"Mom, I'm taking the bus already. I won't melt!" I zip up my hoodie and rush down the stairs. The red front door slams shut behind me, but I stop short. A web stretches from the eave to the rhododendron. The porch light makes the rain droplets glow on the taut strands around the spider hunkered in a ball. I duck under it and hurry into the drizzle.

Gliding on some lip balm, I look back. No one's following me, but I pick up my pace. At the end of our road, I breathe in moist hope and duck into the greenbelt, the wild growth buffering our houses from the street. I push my way through the damp ferns in the predawn darkness. Wiping my hands dry on the back of my jeans, I feel my note for Haddings has worked its way up a bit in my pocket. I shove it down again.

I smile, thinking of how he caught my eye that first day in September when he showed up in study hall. "Don't think of me as your teacher. I'm your poet-in-residence, a grad student on loan from UW," he said.

I closed my copy of *The Bell Jar* and focused on his dark, wavy hair, stubbled jaw, and untucked button-up over a white tee. And then there were his perfect jeans and worn Doc Martens.

With his deep, raspy voice, he dove straight into John Clare's words:

"I hid my love when young till I
Couldn't bear the buzzing of a fly;
I hid my love to my despite
Till I could not bear to look at light;
I dare not gaze upon her face
But left her memory in each place;
Where'er I saw a wild flower lie
I kissed and bade my love good-bye."

At the last word, I got tingles like I was floating in a bubbling hot spring.

"Bro, those words could work on the ladies," said Eric in the back.

"Thank you, PTA, for ponying up for the grad student." Marita smiled, beside me.

Was my ponytail a mess after gym? I tugged out my elastic and let my hair fall in front of my shoulders.

As Haddings' gaze swept the class, I looked down, smoothing the cover of my novel.

"He's so cute," said Marita.

"Whatever." Cydni crossed her arms.

I wrote a note and slid it to her: *Every guy is not your cheater dad.*

"I'm not saying he is," she whispered back. "And enough with the leftover trust issues. I don't have them, okay?"

I raised my brow.

She gave me her most patronizing look. "I'm just saying he's no Luke."

"Are you blind? Besides, anyone outshines my brother." I held up my hand, cutting off her argument. "No matter what you've moaned on about for years."

While Haddings wrote his name on the board, George yawned. "This sucks."

"I know, dude. I can't believe we have to do poetry stuff," said Clayton.

Haddings turned around, and for just a second, he looked straight at me. Blushing, I pulled out my journal. I doodled University of Washington as a possibility for application, right beside Mills.

CHAPTER 2

Haddings

7:10 am

I tilt two sugar packets into my Americano and stir. The Starbucks machine hisses behind me, and I jolt, the steam dissipating my memory of Sarah reading my favorite Byron love poem, "She Walks in Beauty," in front of the class.

After that very first poetry session in September, I had to scramble to reset boundaries when I idiotically told the seniors not to think of me as their teacher. Hearing about it, my professor slayed me. I did know better, and it was arrogant to think I could pull off peer and teacher simultaneously.

I pop a lid on my black coffee. At least my motive to get them to hear poetry was right, and everyone eventually adjusted their view of me ... except for Sarah.

Beside me, a mother in yoga pants and a sweatshirt sets a hot chocolate on the table. "Don't touch," she tells her small son, then turns to answer the barista about her coffee order. When her athletic bag bumps the cup, I lunge and upright it before the hot drink spills on her kid. "Thank you," the woman gushes.

"No problem," I answer. The little boy smiles up at me. "Is Batman your favorite super hero?" I ask, pointing at his hat.

He grins and nods once.

"Me, too."

The mother gets her order. Gripping the two drinks, she scoots her son outside, and even though he's hustled along, he turns and waves. I wave back.

After a sip of coffee, I push out the glass door, too, and run to my car through the rain. The consistency of Seattle winter weather — or Covington, in the suburb — can definitely be counted on. Everyone says I'll get used to it, maybe eventually prefer it to Boulder. Yeah, right. At least rain in town means snow at Crystal Mountain for skiing. Maybe Warren would be up for hitting the slopes over the weekend? Or one of my other friends would go with me? I'm knocked into the present as I dodge a black Mini with pink stripes backing out of the parking slot.

Inside my Mustang, I wipe the rain from my brow and prop my coffee between my legs. Sarah's journal pokes up from among the rest of the students' books in the sack on the floorboard. Her own poetry is amazing. I hesitate but push the journal out of sight. With her talent that distracting, Warren was right to remind me to get my act together. When he stopped by my flat a few weeks ago, he'd said it sounded like the lines were blurred.

"You have to keep her at arm's length," he said.

"No, I know. Of course. Stay professional."

"Always," he emphasized.

"Right, right."

"So, offering a tour of UW to anyone interested was not a good idea."

I dropped my head into my palm.

"*Huge* mistake," Warren said, sipping his IPA.

"Yeah. It was just an eager group of seniors who really wanted an inside look at the campus to see — "

"Everything," he finished for me. "And this girl stayed at your side the entire time and joined you for lunch. Teaching as a sub, I've seen it before. The tour was a bad choice, Jake."

With those words scurrying in my brain, I start my car. Yes, Warren was right, but I've taken care of it now. I'm sure.

Pulling out into traffic, listening to some Pink Floyd, I drive down the dark road toward the school. My headlights illuminate the steady shower skimming the tall firs.

In our last class, I read the poem I intentionally wrote to make the truth clear to Sarah. It hit home so well, she wouldn't meet my eyes afterward. I glance in the rearview. "There can't be anything between us." Gripping the steering wheel, I practice the words in case, by some minute chance, I still need them.

As I shift into third and coast down the hill, I reach for my vibrating phone to check an incoming text. My mom: *Have a nice day*. Ahead, someone exits the upcoming crosswalk, leaving the road clear. I go to tuck my cell into my inside jacket pocket, but I can't find the opening. I look down, letting go of the wheel for just a second.

CHAPTER 3

Sarah

<u>7:16 am</u>

I step out of the greenbelt and wave to Cydni, whose hair is going enormous in the rain. She twists the mass into a messy knot. "Hi," I say, waiting under the streetlight for a truck to pass. It rolls slowly between us then speeds off. I take the moment to flip up my hood against the rain's chill.

"Did you finish Calc, Sarah?" Cydni calls. "Did you, like, get what it was even about? I mean especially the last problems, and oh, that second one was crazy, too."

"Yeah, I got it." I step into the crosswalk. My messenger bag bops against my hip. Down the road, headlights tip over the hill as a car approaches.

"I couldn't figure out most of it," she admits. "Why did I take the class? Why did I let my advisor push me into it?"

"Don't worry. We can go over it." I glance at the car getting closer. "It's not that hard."

"Sure," she says, doubtfully. "Maybe for you it isn't, but I don't have the stupid math gene; you know what I'm saying?"

"You'll get it." Beyond the centerline, I splash into a puddle, soaking my black Chucks. *Sarah, wearing wet socks is the first step to pneumonia* ... Um, no, Mom. Wet socks just feel gross. They're not life threatening. I squish over to the curb.

Cydni pats my arm and points. "You dropped something, Sares. I'll get it for you."

Shoot! "No!" I nudge her back.

"Somebody's touchy," she says, pulling out her phone, protecting it from the drizzle, and checking it.

"No, I mean, it's okay. I got it." Haddings' note teeters on the far edge of the muddy puddle. Holding up my hand, I signal for the car to wait up a sec and dart back into the road, before the note gets ruined.

"Ha! You should see what Kara posted," says Cydni. "Unbelievable."

My fingers curl around the damp folded paper. I shove it into my other back pocket, the one with the closure, and quickly fiddle the snap closed. Why didn't I put it in this one to begin with?

Cydni suddenly shouts, "Sares, the car!"

I straighten, tugging my eyes from her to the rumbling Mustang; my sopping shoes suction the wet street inches from the brilliant headlight. I lurch, flailing my arms and screaming from my gut, "No!"

Bash! Ooooof!

The impact scoops me onto the sizzling hood. I'm sprawled

19

like a broken loose-leaf binder, then shot off the side of the car. I'm flung through the air.

In the dark, through the tiny, stinging raindrops, I jangle apart. The Mustang's red taillights squint smaller and smaller. The wet fir trees' uplifted arms stretch toward me, their pungent needles pricking the air, but I fall, fall, fall. The black asphalt bites my scalp and cracks against my skull.

CHAPTER 4

Haddings

7:20 am

Thump.

My phone slips from my fingers and bounces to the floorboard before I can finish unzipping my jacket pocket. I flit my eyes up and slam the brakes, fishtailing to a stop on the roadside. My cup lid pops off, and hot coffee splashes across my jeans. When I curse and jerk, the cup tips completely.

Over the song "Another Brick in the Wall," I hear someone screaming. I swipe at my wet pants. "What did I hit?" I whisper. "Not a person ..." Looking over my shoulder, I see what could be a body on the edge of the road, maybe twenty-five yards back, and my stomach floats. It's too dark to be sure.

My foot hovers above the accelerator, while the engine growls to fly. *Go! Stay! Go!*

The screaming's louder. "My friend's been hit! Help! Someone help!"

Turning off the car and killing the music, I mumble, "The, the street was dark, and there was rain. I couldn't see through the rain." My chest tightens.

Unbuckling my seat belt, I throw open the door and run back, feeling for my phone in my pocket, but it isn't there; it's back in the car. There's a girl farther up the road screaming into her cell, "911, is this 911?" She braces herself against a tree. "My friend's been hit! She's been hit!"

My shoes punch the wet road. I skid to a stop beside the sprawled body.

"Oh no. No! No! No!" I swear into my fist pressed to my mouth. It's a girl! One shoe is off. Her legs are jumbled, and her pink hoodie is muddy and torn at the sleeve. Perfect white teeth are still behind her open lips. Blond hair is splayed across her eyes, nose, and the shimmering black street, while road rash is burned into her jaw. Blood bubbles from the gouge in her forehead.

"Oh, please, no! It can't be!" I squat, and my quivering fingers sweep the hair from her face. "Sarah?" My own blood rushes in a swoop to my feet, and I teeter. How? How is this possible?

Laying my fingers against her soft neck, I find her pulse. She's breathing. At least she's breathing.

The streetlights pop off as dawn breaks the morning free. Cawing and screeching, a murder of crows fills the evergreens looming above us.

"What, what have I done?" I cry.

"Yes, I'll stay on the line!" The girl on the phone edges closer. It's Cydni, I realize while I'm stripping off my leather jacket and gently covering Sarah.

Nightmarish recognition swoops Cydni's face. "Wait!" She scowls, hunching her shoulders. "Mr. Haddings? You? You ran over my friend? My best friend? What is wrong with you? Get away from her!"

I stand, pitch forward, but then get my feet back under me.

Cydni shrieks and kicks dirt and pebbles at me. "You hit her with your car, you idiot!" In a rage, she swears and stomps in a circle. "What is wrong with you? She was in the crosswalk!" Her eyes dart to Sarah, but she doesn't get closer. "And now she's not moving! *My friend's not moving!*" she says into the phone.

I cover my ears. The girl's crazy dark eyes burn above the spittle spraying out of her mouth. Her wild black bun bobs around her head like a boxer's fist as her words mix and mush.

When her knees give out, she flops down in the patchy grass. "Yes, yes, I'm still here," she bawls. "I can't tell." She looks over. "Yes, she's breathing. Okay. Okay. I won't move her."

"Let me talk." I reach for her phone.

"Back off," she says through clenched teeth.

"Say we need help right now."

"I—did."

I step away from her. Why has no one else driven by? I run into the empty street and turn around and around, waving my arms at no one. "Why aren't the police here yet? Someone, please! Someone, help us!" Only crows shrilly answer.

Cydni's crouched, sniveling and repeating, "Uh huh, Uh huh," over and over again.

I rush back to Sarah and kneel in the rain.

"Don't touch her," Cydni yells.

"I'm helping!" I narrow my eyes, and she does the same, but she doesn't try to stop me from tucking my jacket closer around

Sarah's neck. I sit on my haunches and rock over her. "How could I have hit her? How? What kind of cosmic dark humor is this?" My breath breaks in and out. "Not Sarah!" I beg.

"It is her, you spaz," Cydni interjects.

Pressing my sleeve to Sarah's head, my wrist moistens as she bleeds quickly through the material. I float above the scene in a stupor while my joints solidify in the dampness and my muscles cramp.

"I hear them!" Cydni says into the phone. She jumps up, waving at the ambulance and police coming down the road.

"Quick, over here. Here!" I call out.

In only a few moments, medics swoop in, and I'm pulled away by a cop who escorts me to his car. Hands grip my arms, keeping me upright. Slack-jawed, I can't make sense of his questions or even see Sarah anymore.

Across the street, police interview Cydni. She's flapping her arms around, pointing at me. A block away, another cop diverts a school bus down a side road, along with the gathering morning traffic.

CHAPTER 5

Sarah

7:41 am

My eyelids are leaden. Pain scoops at my skull. So much ... pain. Think ... think of something else. Something good. Think of good ... ness. It's like I can almost hear Haddings' voice right now. Haddings ...

I drift in the memory of poetry class. Flipping through Haddings' collections. Copying favorites ... reading aloud Shel Silverstein ... and William Shakespeare.

Shiki's haiku swirls up:

Nightlong in the cold
that monkey sits conjecturing
how to catch the moon.

Haddings' hand lingers on the edge of my journal. He reads over my shoulder, his heat hovering around me.

Reality slashes the dream, and the cold street burns my cheek. My head throbs like it's pumpkin-sized. I open my eyes to small wheels rolling toward me. Feet.

"She's regained consciousness," a woman says on my right.

A man slips a cuff off my arm. My fingertips tingle. "Bypass Valley. She needs an airlift to Harborview in Seattle."

Wait. Stop! Stop everything! What is going on? I, I need to get to school. I need to go—but this woman tosses a jacket aside and unzips my hoodie. Scissors slice my shirt. What—is—going—on?

Now she's cutting my jeans! I try to reach for the poem in my pocket, but my arms lie still at my sides.

"No, don't," I shout, but it's only a gargled whisper. "Stop! Stop it—" Someone's going to see! I need to cover myself, but I can't. Why? Why can't I move? And who are these people? Someone, help me!

A blanket covers my underwear and bra. "Why did you cut off my clothes? What are you doing to me?" I whimper. One medic checks a monitor while the other steps away.

Suddenly, I can lift my head, but pain smashes my skull like a Cyclops with a bludgeon. I look to the side and vomit. Munched Cheerios swirl against the curb.

Ugh. Please, don't look! Nobody look at it!

"You were hit by a car," the female answers and wipes my lips with gauze.

What? What did she say?

"We're checking you over." She shines a little flashlight into my eyes. "Concussion." A board is set beside me.

26

Thump, thump, thump thrums my skull. A giant collar gets strapped around my neck. "Please! Don't move my head," I beg. "Please," I say through tears.

"Ready. Now." The man and woman lift me onto the board.

I retch again. The puke splatters onto the road, covering the blood.

The paramedics tightly strap my legs and chest. Lights laser my eyes and zing off the pale sunshine cutting through the trees. My stomach creeps, and I vomit one more time.

CHAPTER 6

Haddings

At some point, someone retrieved my jacket from the roadside, where a medic had tossed it. With it now balled in my hands, I shiver beside the police car. The rain's only misting as the sun streams more strongly through the firs, and my wet clothes cling like plastic wrap over microwaved pizza. Vapor steams up from the road, the white tendrils magnifying the red flares and blue police car lights. All the vehicles jammed into this space are either helping Sarah or waiting for answers from me. Everything pulses, including the blood swelling the vein in my temple.

Still not able to see Sarah, I grab the moment when the cop turns and talks to the investigator. I weave my way to the ambulance. My fingers touch the hood. "Hemorrhaging," one medic

28

says to the other inside the unit. "Airlift request to Harborview accepted."

Before I can catch a glimpse of her, the policeman catches up to me. "Mr. Haddings?" He turns me around.

"I'm sorry. I'm sorry," I say as he leads me all the way back to my car, still sitting in the road, right where I stopped after I hit Sarah.

"At the point of impact, were you wearing your seat belt?" he asks, walking around the side and peering inside my Mustang.

"Yes. Yes, I was." I lean against the car trunk to steady my legs.

He straightens and tugs his hat lower on his brow. "And your estimated speed?"

As the ambulance drives past, I irrationally lunge to follow it on foot, but the cop grabs my arm. "Mr. Haddings, your speed at the impact?"

"Um. Maybe thirty?" I glance at the 25 mph sign over his shoulder.

"And you had your eyes on the road but didn't see the pedestrian?"

"Yes, well, I looked down for only a second, but I didn't see her afterward. It was dark and raining, you know?"

His pen scratches across his paper. "You weren't on your phone or texting?"

"No, I was not texting. One came in, but I didn't answer it." I rest my palm on the cold trunk. Everything is careening off center.

An investigator photographs my car and the street as my legs buckle. I stay squatting, leaning against the bumper. Tears burst up, and suddenly I'm bawling. I'm a teacher, someone in charge of protecting his students, not hitting them with his car. What is wrong with me?

The cop opens my door, helps me up, and walks me over to sit.

"Thank you," I blurt, collapsing on the damp coffee-drenched seat. I toss my bloody, dirty jacket into the back and grab the towel from my gym bag. After drying my face, I lift up and squirm the cloth over my seat, trying to smooth it flat beneath me. "Will you be taking me in now?"

He raises an eyebrow. "You ready?"

"No, no," I say, even though jail is what I deserve. They've got to be afraid I'll run after what I just did. Will I? Or hit someone else?

The policeman slips his pen into his pocket. "No, we won't be taking you anywhere. Not now. Criminal charges may be filed by the prosecutor, or there could be a civil suit from the parents, but you'd be notified." He adjusts his hat again against the morning glare. "We can let you go after the investigator finishes her work. Sit tight for a bit, Mr. Haddings."

"All right." I lean the side of my face against the steering wheel and watch as he returns to his cruiser. He stops and talks to another couple of officers. Dazed, I'm motionless while all of these people document the scene of my crime. I just don't understand why, why they aren't taking me in.

As the coffee stench nauseates me even more, I fish out my water bottle from my bag. I take a swig hoping to settle my stomach. Leaning out of my car, I tip the bottle and douse Sarah's blood from my sleeve, rubbing the material until finally, there's only a faint pink swatch left. It refuses to completely disappear, holding me to what I've done.

I find my phone near the brake pedal. It's vibrating nearly nonstop as texts shoot in from my friends: Warren, Charline, Larry. I toss it onto the other seat, knowing the story has spread over social media already. Sarah is my focus right now. I just need to get to Sarah to make sure she is all right.

Overhead, a red-and-white helicopter thumps past. It's got to be meeting her at the emergency airlift. The rotor blades slice my guts.

CHAPTER 7

Sarah

There's an incredible noise and strong pulse. With a colossal effort, I lift my eyelids and whimper.

A medic smiles down at me and adjusts his big headset. "You're going to get help!" he shouts. He checks an IV bag hanging next to me. I struggle to sit up, but straps press against my arms and legs. "Lie still now. You're in a helicopter!" he says. Clouds shimmy past the little window.

A helicopter? Wasn't I getting put into an ambulance? The Cyclops in my head crunches my skull. I squeeze my eyes shut and break into a total body sweat.

Get me out of here! How can I be in a helicopter when I'm afraid to fly in a regular plane?

My mind rides the ripping pain on spin cycle. Am I ... losing consciousness? Remembering? I'm chatting with Cydni about Haddings.

"It's not a crush, Cydni," I told her at our sleepover during holiday break.

"Yeah, right. That's what you say."

"It's not." I beaned her with my stuffed panda.

She deflected him with her elbow and laughed. "Whatever it is, you need to be super careful, or people are going to start talking. Just imagine what they'd be saying about you behind your back."

"There's nothing to talk about." I pulled the covers to my chin and looked down at her as she got into her old Hello Kitty sleeping bag on my bedroom floor. After I clicked off the light, I whispered into the darkness, "I know it sounds stupid, but Haddings is, like, opening up the world to me or something." I waited for her to answer, but she didn't. "You know, through the poetry, how he explains the symbols and meanings. It's amazing to hear what all those poets have had to say. It's the same stuff I think about and more."

"Uh huh, and ..."

"And there is no 'and.'" I paused, then admitted my secret into the silence. "And Haddings makes me feel beautiful when he looks at me."

She sighed. "Sarah, you are beautiful and always have been. I don't even know why you'd say that."

"No, I mean seriously beautiful—to a man. Not some high school guy just interested in what he can get from me, like Seth or Dwayne."

"Okay, they were jerks. And I have to say, right here, that Luke would never treat me like those guys treated you. Never."

"We were talking about Haddings, Cydni."

"I know that. I was just saying—"

"And Haddings is brilliant. He could teach me so much."

"Sure he could," she jibed. "He could teach you so much."

"That's *not* what I meant, Cydni."

She snickered, and her sleeping bag rustled.

"I've never had a class like his before."

"Yeah, I get that. And I hear you saying it's not a crush, but then I see you going all crazy, talking about switching from Mills to UW. What is that about?"

"That has nothing to do with him," I lied to us both.

"Sure, Sarah." She zipped her bag. "Just know, if anything did happen between you and Haddings and anyone found out, there'd be serious fallout. Do you know what I mean?"

I rolled away from her.

"You know I've never liked him, for a bazillion reasons, but it's not a game. You could get him fired, so think about it. This isn't a little fun with some guy, Sarah."

I fluffed my pillow. "It's just so stupid when I'm turning eighteen next month, you know?"

"It still wouldn't matter as long as he's our teacher."

"But wasn't it amazing when he recited Plato?"

"Plato?"

I said the sweet words.

> *"My child—Star—you gaze at the stars,*
> *and I wish I were the firmament*
> *that I might watch you with many eyes."*

The helicopter drops, crashing my memory. As the door slides open, the Cyclops rolls. The sun sizzles my eyes, and the gurney jerks and bounces. While I groan and cry, my bound chest thrums under the pressure of the thumping blades whirling above us.

Double doors whoosh open. Antiseptic fries my nose, and my jaw quivers. "I have to get to school," I spew to the person running next to me.

"Now, now." The woman smiles. Her gray curls clasp her lined face. "I'm sure your teachers will all be very concerned and understanding. How could they not for a beautiful young lady like you?"

From the darkest bend of my brain, words twist and turn, rushing from me. "I, I need my mom!"

"She'll be here soon, sweetie," the woman says softly. "You rest now."

My lips blubber. "But my head hurts so bad. I really need my mother."

"Of course you do." We stop, and an elevator dings. "You've had a very hard morning."

8:24 am

"Sarah. Sarah, stay with me. Focus."

Who is this woman? Where's the other, nice one?

"Sarah, the CAT scan makes it feel like you're wetting yourself," she says, "and that's normal."

I gape at her.

35

"Don't worry. You won't be." She spins the silver rings on her fingers. "Is your pain medication taking effect yet?"

"I don't ... know." Fear creeps around my shoulders but then flops off. What is there to be afraid of? The fresh blanket poofs warmth onto my face. "I'm so sleepy," I say. "Dreamy ... dreamy, dreamy."

"Sounds like it's starting to work."

"May — be?"

The lady moves out of the room.

"Hold your breath for fifteen seconds," the machine says.

Hиииp.

Don't pee. Don't pee.

CHAPTER 8

Haddings

As the time dragged, I did text the department head at the high school and told her I wouldn't be in today. I suggested the kids use the session as a study hall and gave no explanation for not coming in. It was ridiculous to think of teaching, but I couldn't get those students off my mind. They are my responsibility, too, and I hope I'll have a chance to make up the material at some point ... that is, if I still have an opportunity to teach.

The cops slowly route traffic through one lane. In the side mirror, I watch someone pull up in a blue Volkswagen Beetle and pick up Cydni. She glowers at me as she rolls past in the car.

After what seems like forever, a policeman returns and says I'm free to go.

"Thank you," I say. With a trembling hand, I shove the key

into the ignition. Starting my car, my stomach turns over faster than the engine when I pull into traffic.

9:06 am

Oblivious to the drive, I'm suddenly in a parking spot in the packed hospital garage. Adrenaline flying, I yank up the emergency brake. It should have taken thirty-five minutes or so to get here. No, it should have been worse than that with the morning commute. How fast was I speeding? I could have hit someone else. I groan and shake my head to clear it.

Sarah's helicopter flight was probably like ten minutes, tops. At least they got her here as fast as possible. I turn from the thought that she needed it and cram on a baseball cap. Stretching past my leather coat, I nab my denim jacket from the backseat and yank it on.

Hesitating a second, I riffle through the bag of kids' journals and pull Sarah's little notebook out; it's something that makes it seem like she's close and all right. I tuck it into my pocket. "Okay." I take a deep breath, hoping to slow my pulse. Just find out what's going on and then you can figure out what you need to do. Keep a level head so you're ready to react clearly to whatever has happened. "Okay," I gulp.

After locking up, I jog to the elevator and an obvious realization hits me. "No one in Sarah's family is going to want to see me after what I did. No one," I mutter. I push the up button. But I still have to know how she is, and it's still my responsibility to see if there's anything I can do. Right?

"Nothing," the attendant says, "if you aren't immediate family." He sits behind the high, orange desk, which makes this feel more like a hotel than a hospital, and clicks his pen.

"You can't tell me anything?" I ask.

"Nothing."

I walk across the shiny floor and drop into a maroon chair in the corner of what I think is the main lobby. Someone from the family is bound to show up soon.

My phone buzzes with a text. The department head's cryptic message acknowledges she got mine. Great. I won't think any more about it. I can handle the remaining high school issues and also the university later.

Scrolling down, there's my mom's text to have a good day. Yeah, right. With my thumbs poised to reply at least to her, I glance up and notice the no cell phone signs. I tap off my phone's power and wrap my arms around my waist while staring at the little plant sitting in the center of the small side table. Miscellaneous families and friends pause around the nearby tall pillars, orienting themselves and making plans before the hospital swallows them from sight.

After a stream of people are processed into the system, a guy tears through the electric doors, his sneakers squeaking. "I need to find my sister." He slaps the curved reception counter. "Sarah McCormick."

Bingo. The attendant checks the computer and points to a map beneath the counter's glass surface.

"Um, where is that?" the kid asks.

The man smiles and clicks his pen. "Down this hall, take

the elevator to Wing C. Stepping out, take a right, go past the chapel and gift shop, then turn at the second left, where you'll see another bank of elevators. From there, go down to the basement. Make one more right, and follow the signs to the waiting room for friends and family of emergency patients. Be sure to take a moment and appreciate the big fish tank, which is brand new and lovely. That waiting room is where a doctor will let you know how your sister is doing. My system shows she's having a CAT scan right now. Okay then?"

The brother shoves his hand through his buzzed blond hair. "You're serious?"

"Is there a problem?" A patronizing smile. "Let me explain one more time."

The kid listens to the instructions again and then takes off before I can decide whether to introduce myself.

I hustle after him, but he's already out of sight. I find the elevators and dart into an open one, but there's no button to indicate Wing C. A woman in a white coat and a surgery cap enters.

"I'm looking for the basement of Wing C?" I say.

She holds down the open button. "The elevator you need is at the end of the hall."

"Thanks." I rush out, find the elevator, and make my way past the chapel and gift shop, hurrying all the way to the right floor. I nearly stumble into the brother and maybe his mom, standing at another desk. The thin woman tucks her straight brown hair behind her ear and clutches her purse to her chest. All in black, it looks as if she's already mourning. I take a step forward to say hello, until I hear her say, "I could kill the person who did this to your sister."

Slipping into an adjacent, empty waiting room, I take a seat in a slick tan chair and flip open a *National Geographic*. My intuition was right—there's no way Sarah's mom wants to lay eyes on me right now. It would be no help at all, a detriment even.

"Do you understand, Mrs. McCormick?" the attendant asks her. "We will not let you see Sarah if you can't control your emotions. We can't have you upsetting her."

Another reason for me to stay out of sight.

"I won't," the mom says, looking down and signing a form. And another. "This is her brother, Luke. He won't either."

The employee pushes more paperwork across the desk. "This form allows the hospital to update any friends who might call. Do you want to sign it?" she asks.

I peek over the top of the shiny page. She does sign. Perfect! I could go home and call in for the status updates if I wanted. My grip tightens on the magazine, and I don't get up.

Can you tell I'm here, Sarah? As your teacher and the one who caused all this, I care for you. I bite my lip and close my eyes. *What have I done to your future? If, if you have one.* I swallow my tears. *What have I done to mine?*

"I have to see my daughter. Please!" says her mom.

"Follow me." The woman stands and leads them past the room I'm in. "Sarah's finishing her second CAT scan," the woman's voice carries. "But a police officer has arrived, and he can give you details about the accident."

My strength slips while my ears catch fire trying to hear anything else, but the group has moved out of range. I set aside the magazine and lean forward into my hands. Freed, my tears drip through my fingers.

Just when I manage to get it together again, I hear them

41

returning. I snatch a tissue from the box on the side table and swipe my eyes and nose.

"Can you believe that, Luke?" the mother says, stopping right outside the small waiting room. "Thirty-five in a twenty-five?"

"It's crazy. But, Mom? Mom? What do you think Sarah looks like, being hit and thrown so far? Do you think it's bad? Like really bad? Creepy? What will everyone at school say when they see her? Mom?"

She doesn't answer. "Mrs. McCormick?" A nurse comes from the other direction.

"Yes?"

"I can take you to see Sarah. This way, please."

As soon as they are out of sight, I jump up and follow at a distance, until … there. Beyond the three of them, a stretcher sits in the hall strung up with IVs and tubes and who knows what else. Sarah? A nurse monitors the attachments.

I take a step and stop, then one more and hesitate. My legs freeze so close to the mother's rigid spine. Is this her last chance to talk to Sarah? I can't take that from her by putting myself into the situation. The brother ducks into the large waiting room just beyond, without stopping at the gurney. I turn at the nearby corner and wait, close enough to overhear.

"Sarah! Oh, my baby! Oh, Sarah!" Mrs. McCormick cries.

CHAPTER 9

Sarah

9:32 am

Mom? My mom's here? She blurs and shifts.

"There you go, Sarah." She nudges the blankets close to my chin. Ahhhh. The warmth settles around me like a hug. She's here! Everything's going to be okay now. "Hiiiii, Mommy."

"Oh, sweetheart." She leans over and kisses my cheek.

I blink slowly. "Mom, tell this nurse I need to go to school." My eyes close. At school I can give Haddings my poem. Then I can go to UW.

"School's not important right now, Sarah. Don't you worry about it, because, honey, it doesn't matter. Just rest, because everything is going to be okay."

"But I want—"

"Sarah, please. Rest. Rest, honey."

"Mills is an all-women's school," I sing. And he won't be there. Nope. Nope. Nope. "Mom, I'll just chill while you take care of everything … 'cause I'm super sleepy, Mommy."

She touches my cheek.

"Oh, but I am needin' a note for school, 'cause I'm late, I think. And … could ya bring me that other shirt you said would look better? Okaaaaay."

CHAPTER 10

Haddings

9:34 am

Covering my mouth with my hands, I absorb the sound of Sarah's voice, relish it, even if she's loopy. I stare at my wavering reflection in the huge cobalt vase in the hall recess. Maybe everything is going to be okay?

A skinny doctor darts past with a clipboard, his jacket flapping behind him like wings. "Mrs. McCormick? I need to speak with you." His Indian accent is soft but urgent. "Please, step over here. Take no anxiety now. The nurse will attend to Sarah."

The two of them move into my line of sight below the set of fluorescent lights. They stop in profile to me, both intensely engaged. "Please, tell me how she is," Mrs. McCormick says, her hands at her neck.

"Sarah has suffered severe head trauma. Do you see the blood pooling in this most recent CAT scan? It is the white area."

She stands there, frozen before the image.

"We've determined the blood puddle is continuing to grow and pressing more and more against Sarah's brain. Left untreated, permanent damage will result. We now have less than twenty minutes to relieve the pressure."

Whoa. My stomach flops and fizzles. I lean against the tan wall and take a deep breath.

The doctor continues. "The staff is preparing for brain surgery. We'll be shaving the front portion of her head to reach the effected quadrant. Is everything clear, Mrs. McCormick?"

There's no answer. Blood, pooling, shaving, brain surgery. Sarah's mom shouldn't be alone right now. Does she have a husband? I don't even know.

I start to walk to her. One step. Two.

"Who would do this to my child?" she says, voice rising.

"Please take control of yourself, Mrs. McCormick."

I scuttle back and sink into a squat, pretending I'm retying my boot. She'll totally lose it if I appear suddenly. I can't distract and delay her decisions.

"Mrs. McCormick, time is life. You need to authorize the procedure, and at the same moment, you must understand that the surgery may or may not be successful."

"May not?" she repeats.

"Correct, but we have no other choice. The surgery is imperative, Mrs. McCormick. Sign here. And here. This page. And the next. Initial here, here, and here. No. Don't bother filling in the relation line. It isn't necessary."

"I will sign that I am her mother, do you understand? In all of this, I am still her mother!"

He rustles the papers together. "All right then," he says. "The nurse will show you to the waiting area. We'll let you know as soon as Sarah comes out of surgery."

He steps away, leaving Mrs. McCormick holding the pen. The one she used to let them cut open Sarah's skull.

CHAPTER 11

Sarah

"So you're going to have a little surgery," a woman says.

Another nurse? "I am?"

"Yes. But you won't feel a thing. You'll sleep through the whole experience."

"Okey-dokey. Just … be very, very … careful." I sigh. "That's what Mommy always says. Always, always, al …" Wait. Should I be afraid?

A chill runs through the tube from the new IV bag and freezes me like an ice cube.

CHAPTER 12

Haddings

I step into the nearby bathroom and furiously splash my face with water. Okay, think. They are going to perform surgery because there's hope. I rip a scratchy brown paper towel from the machine and dry my face. They wouldn't operate if there was no hope, therefore it's possible Sarah may survive, recover, and continue to live as well as she ever has. We could both recover from this disaster.

I come out of the bathroom and stand in the hall before a painting of a sunset. People walk by with hardly a glance at me. Everyone must be preoccupied with their own tragedies.

When I hear the anesthesiologist arrive, I move closer to the corner again.

Sarah's mom says, "I insist you add an antinausea drug to her anesthetic. That was helpful during my foot surgery."

"Yes, we can do that," is the response. Something buzzes, and it sounds like the anesthesiologist starts to leave. "The nurse will return momentarily," he says.

I peek around the corner to see the set of double doors at the end of the hall swing shut. Mrs. McCormick fusses over the gurney, so I can't see Sarah, especially with the blankets piled so high.

"Your hand is cold, sweetie," the mom says. "Oh, I can't believe they just have you in a hallway! Hold on, honey. Hold on." Mrs. McCormick lays her head on Sarah's chest.

I withdraw again and bite the inside of my cheek. I wiggle my toes in my boots to get some feeling back into my numb feet.

"You okay?" A big male attendant pauses his fast stride.

I jump. "Oh, yeah. Thanks." I swipe at my nose.

"Maybe find a place to sit it out? There's the surgery waiting room," he says.

"Yeah, thanks."

He rushes on around the corner. "Sarah McCormick?" he asks.

I hear wheels rolling down the hallway, double doors swinging shut, and a mother's moan.

CHAPTER 13

Sarah

9:46 am

My mom's gone. Where'd she go?

This room's too bright. Where am I? I squint. Something keeps my head from turning, but a few people cluster in my line of sight. They all have their backs to me.

"You are going to have a very funny haircut, young lady," someone says behind me.

What? What does that mean? Wait, no! I don't want my hair cut. My lip quivers, and tears spill from my eyes. My breath jerks in and out, but I can't get my mouth to answer.

Does Haddings like short hair? What will my mom say? She likes my hair long.

A sliver of reality snakes into my foggy head. "I'm having

brain surgery?" my voice squeaks out. No one turns around to answer me. Not one single person.

Am, am I going to die? My tears flow off my face. God, help me, I pray. God, please!

Finally someone comes over to my side. Is it a man? The eyes stare at me, above the blue face mask. Regardless of my tears, there's no reaction from this person whatsoever.

Anger boils through me. "I'm not a freaking specimen," I spit, wondering if the words actually came out.

The person tilts his head to the side and just keeps staring.

A mask drops over my nose. "Now," someone explains, "I want you to count backward from one hundred."

Pairs of eyes swim around my head. There are tugs on my arms. My toes. The holey ceiling tiles wave at me. Big round lights swoop past.

Stop! I don't want to have surgery. I don't want to die! Someone, help me! I try to shout but fail.

"Sarah, count for me."

Count? My eyes slide closed, and this stupid rhyme jingles through my cracked skull as I drift away.

Ninety-nine bottles of beer on the wall.

CHAPTER 14

Haddings

9:47 am

Keeping my head down, I walk right by Sarah's mom. She's mumbling something about returning to the desk down the hall for more information. I start to reach out, take her hand, and beg her to forgive me, but I stop my selfishness. She storms off in the opposite direction.

My heavy legs carry me into the large surgery waiting room that Luke went into earlier. The chairs are placed in little groupings and create privacy. There. Luke's in the corner with Cydni and an older woman. The latter looks at me, but I keep walking since I've never seen her before. I'd definitely remember those red eyeglasses.

If only Cydni doesn't look up. Don't look; don't look, I chant, and her head doesn't budge. I drop into a chair on the opposite side of the huge fish tank filled with coral fans and saltwater fish. An additional potted palm even blocks this cluster of chairs from the rest of the room.

If I bend just a bit, I can see Cydni, Luke, and the woman through the tank glass, between the swaying kelp leaves, above the conch shell. The three look a bit distorted, but I can hear their voices carry over the top of the aquarium. Perfect. I could stay here all day, and no one would notice. Even the volunteer greeter is out of sight. I shift and see both females are completely absorbed in what Luke's talking about.

"Yeah. I couldn't stand to see her like that. My mom might be mad I left her out there with Sarah, but I couldn't deal, you know?" He looks at Cydni. "I know that sounds lame, but it was horrible even from a distance. So bloody. So much gore."

"Oh," I moan under my breath while a huge angelfish swims past.

Cydni reassures him. "I know your mom is fine that you came in here. Believe me, I know how bad Sares looks, so your mom will understand. She probably didn't even notice you left."

"Yeah. Right." He bobs his head. "She was totally focused on my sister."

The older woman jumps. "Should I go to her?"

"No," Luke says quickly. "She would want privacy, and my dad should be here any second."

What a relief; Sarah has a father, and Mrs. McCormick will have support. I squeeze my brow under the bill of my cap.

The woman nods and resettles in the chair. "Well, whether you stayed out there or not, it's good you are here to support your sister and mom, Luke. I couldn't believe it when Cydni called." She sniffs and dabs her eyes.

"Yeah. It's tough, man." Luke rubs his palms on his knees. "Can you believe I almost didn't get here myself?"

"Why?" Cydni asks. "What happened? I mean, tell us everything."

"Well, my phone was crammed with texts by the time I pulled up at school. Before I could read even one, everyone was running across the parking lot to tell me there had been an accident."

"I can imagine," Cydni nods. "I was talking to 911, or I totally would have called you."

"Yeah, I'm sure. So, anyway, I didn't even turn off my truck. Someone yelled out that Sarah was airlifted here. I just backed up and took off. I was driving so fast that when I hit the ramp onto I-5, I pulled a 360 on the wet road."

"No way!" she and the woman gasp.

"Can you believe that, Mom?" Cydni asks the woman, who has now gone pale.

"Yes, way," says Luke. "It was crazy. But I straightened her out without hitting a thing. It was unbelievable. Don't tell my mom."

"That's the last thing she needs to hear," the mother agrees.

"So, what else about the accident, Cydni? What haven't you told me?" Luke asks.

"Well, I told you it was Haddings who hit her. That stupid poetry intern. I can't stand him."

I slouch and pull the collar up on my jacket.

"Why's that?" her mother asks.

Cydni shrugs. "I don't know, really. It's just that all the girls go on and on because they are crushing on him, when he's not even that cute. Basically, he's arrogant and self-absorbed. I don't get why everyone likes him, but whatever. None of that really matters anymore, since he ran down my best friend, you know? There's a perfect reason to hate him now."

There's a recollection on Luke's face. "Oh, I know what guy you're talking about! I mean, I've heard about him."

My hands shake as I pick up a pamphlet and hold it in front of my face. Arrogant? Cydni's and Luke's horrible impressions of me drone on.

"Right," says Cydni. "The one who organized and led the UW tour. You should have seen all the girls who went."

"I remember that," says Luke. "Didn't Sarah go, too?"

"Oh, yeah. She told me she stuck close to hear his every word. Even got to sit at his table for lunch in the dining hall."

Luke nods. "Well, she's really into UW, right?"

"Mm hmm," says Cydni.

"Man, she's going to freak when she hears Haddings was the one who hit her. I mean she likes him, doesn't she?"

Cydni tilts her head. "You could say that."

My face burns as I realize Cydni knows of Sarah's attraction to me. She knows, and with how much she dislikes me, what might she choose to spin in the future? I can't, can't think of this now. I swallow. All that matters is Sarah's state; the surgery is what matters.

"Well, I could tear his head off." Luke thumps his heel on the carpet.

"After me," says Cydni, crossing her arms.

"Now, you two," Cydni's mom interrupts. "Let's focus on the positive, not this negative energy, all right?"

Their conversation peters, and I'm swallowed up by the other conversations around me. Moms and dads, kids and grandparents, all wearing worry on their faces, holding it in their clasped hands and curved backs.

Looking over the top of the pamphlet on heart attack prevention, I see a man stride into the room. He's tall, with curly, receding light red hair. A Boeing name tag dangles from his neck. "Dad!" says Luke. He hustles over to him and exchanges an awkward hug.

"Finally," I whisper.

"It's going to be all right, Luke," the dad says. "Oh, Cydni and her mother, Chantelle, are here?"

"Yeah. Cydni was there when it happened, Dad." Luke leads his father to where they are sitting. "Did you see Sares or Mom out in the hall?"

He shakes his head. "No, it was empty."

"Okay, well, Dad, listen. I heard a little bit earlier. They're doing brain surgery, because some teacher hit Sares with his car. It was this poetry guy. This is super serious, Dad. Hemorrhaging and stuff. She — she might not be all right!"

I massage my temples.

As the reality starts to dawn on Mr. McCormick's face, his wife steps into the room. She stands in the doorway, slightly swaying in her sleek black boots. Most everyone stops and looks over at her, but it's her husband who rushes to her side now. For just a second, she curls against his chest.

"Sarah is going to be fine, Janet," he says.

She jerks away, her brows squeeze close. "Mark, listen — "

"Let's keep perspective. We don't need any added drama."

My eyes widen.

He keeps going. "Have you seen Sarah or the doctor?"

"Yes, Mark." Janet flips her hair back from her face. "Sarah's having brain surgery. I signed the form to allow the surgery."

He takes a step back. "Why? Why did you do that?"

"Because otherwise she'd have permanent brain damage or die."

My heart skips and drops.

"God, please no," Mark prays, looking up.

"So," Janet continues, "don't stand there and tell me not to be dramatic, and everything's going to be fine! Wake up"—she pokes him in the chest—"and deal with it."

He lifts his palms. "What? What are you talking about? I'm dealing with this. I'm right here!"

"Sure, Mark. It took you how long to get here? I left messages everywhere."

"I was driving and couldn't answer my phone. As soon as I got to the office, I turned around and headed straight here."

I wipe the sweat from my upper lip. Man. What would she say to me?

She looks up at her husband and closes her eyes a second. "All right, look. It doesn't matter now. I just know I asked you and I asked Luke to drive …" Her shoulders shudder. "If you had only …"

"Janet, we can escalate the accusations or focus on Sarah." He reaches out and barely touches her arm. When she flinches, he drops his hand, but he does lock eyes with folks around the waiting room. One by one they go back to the games on their phones, their magazines, and their books, or they just find their laps as interesting as I suddenly do. Even the little girl across the way starts singing quietly to her baby doll again.

Out of the corner of my eye, I see the two parents make their

58

way over to Luke, Cydni, and Chantelle. First thing, Janet gets right up in Cydni's face. "Don't you cry," she says. "Do you hear me?" Her voice is needlelike. "They won't let me see Sarah after the surgery if I'm crying. So don't you cry and make me cry. Don't you!"

Cydni blinks fast and licks the tear off her cheek. "I won't, Mrs. McCormick."

Chantelle lurches up, unsteady on her chubby legs. She bumps her way past a couple to get into the bathroom. It's easy to hear her sobbing over the running faucet.

Janet rolls her lips inward and shoves her hand into Luke's. It's like she holds on to him for Sarah's life.

I weave my trembling fingers together and squeeze them still.

"I can't believe the guy's not even in jail," Luke mutters. "I want to smash his face with my fist. Run him down with my truck."

I deserve it.

"Enough, Luke," says Mark.

CHAPTER 15

Haddings

As the hours tick past, my mind replays every second before and after the accident. I try to piece the actual event together, but I didn't see it, so I really don't know what happened. It's a relief, actually, as I can't imagine dealing with what Cydni saw, it playing on repeat in her mind. But then if I had seen, I could have swerved, I bet.

Then my head fills with images of what they are doing to Sarah now: cutting and peeling back her scalp, sawing her skull open, cracking it back, suctioning blood, burning the leaking vessels closed, closing her up like the hood of a car, rolling her scalp back into place, and stitching her closed like that doll the child is hugging over there. The girl swings her legs, pats her baby's head, then chews on its ear.

My stomach tosses about, but it's suddenly Luke who runs to the bathroom and pukes.

"Are you okay?" Mark calls from the door.

"Uh huh."

Mark goes to Cydni and Chantelle. "I want to thank you both for coming."

They nod and half smile. The mom pushes up her glasses and answers, "We love Sarah, and we want you to know we are here for you."

Mark nods like a bobblehead doll. Eventually, he sits down again and starts praying softly. "Have mercy on my baby girl. Have mercy. Preserve this precious life you've shared with us, and help me have mercy on that grad student."

I cough as quietly as I can, startled at this man's kindness, or at least his good intention. Maybe there will be a right moment for me to speak to him, accept responsibility, and offer help.

It's an incredible mercy no one has seen me behind this fish tank. I scoot even farther behind the palm, thankful everyone has tunnel vision.

Janet pinches the bridge of her nose and studies the CAT scan in her lap. The paper shudders as she folds it and slips it into her purse. Chantelle puts an arm around her while Janet stares straight ahead and whispers in a super eerie way, "I'm disappearing without a speck of control. All I can do is beg. Bless the surgeons. Bless the anesthesiologist. Bless the nurses. Bless the room. Bless my daughter's brain. Bless the instruments." Then, she starts the list over.

"You okay?" Cydni asks Luke when he comes out and sits down beside her.

He pops an Altoids and shrugs like it's no big deal. "It all got to me, I guess." He offers Cydni a mint then pockets the tin.

"You love her is why. That's what it is," she says. "I'm sure of it, you know?"

He blushes, but says, "Yeah, you're right."

"So you think everyone's heard Haddings hit Sarah?" Cydni asks.

"I'm sure. Between texts and stuff. Definitely."

Cydni looks away from him and mutters to herself, "Thankfully, it's over before it started."

"What?" Luke asks.

"Nothing."

Luke pulls out his cell. "I wish we had reception down here."

"No kidding."

From my jacket pocket, I tug out Sarah's poetry journal and find looking at it suddenly seems almost too intimate. She takes the class so seriously, it's as if this book holds her heart. I flip to her last entry, Anna Akhmatova's poem.

Everything Promised Him to Me

Everything promised him to me:
the fading amber edge of the sky,
and the sweet dreams of Christmas,
and the wind at Easter, loud with bells,

and the red shoots of the grapevine,
and waterfalls in the park,
and two large dragonflies
on the rusty iron fencepost.

And I could only believe
that he would be mine

as I walked along the high slopes,
the path of burning stones.

The journal quivers in my palm. Is this how she felt about me? Or is there another student she's interested in? I can only hope.

The poem taps at my own heart, and I lock the door on the sudden rush of feelings. It's exactly what Warren said: "She can be beautiful, intelligent, even gifted, but you can't allow yourself to get involved. Stay professional."

Right. Absolutely right. I'm just hyperaware, feeling sentimental because I'm the teacher ... who hit her. I slouch a second, losing my view of Sarah's family and friends, and lean my head against the cold fish tank. I stare down the small blue lobster raising his claws and skittering in the corner. Will Sarah walk again?

The angelfish flits past the kelp, dislodging a small piece of a dead fish, which bobs up to the top of the tank. Manslaughter slams my mind, and my pulse speeds. Come on. Stop! Stop freaking out. I bend over, get my head lower. List what you know. List it. Sarah is in surgery, and she's still alive. We think. They are operating because there is hope. Both of her parents are praying. I heard her in the hallway. She was speaking.

Rising up, I watch the angelfish circle aimlessly. Matt Nathanson's lyrics for "Car Crash" ring in my head: *I wanna feel the car crash, 'Cause I'm dyin' on the inside.*

No. No one is dying here. Especially not Sarah.

12:11 pm

When Janet gets up to check at the desk for news, this strange guy sits down with the others. His greasy hair strands swing as

63

he tells jokes. His head jerks when he talks. What is he thinking? Doesn't he realize it's bad taste to laugh in a place like this?

"And then the duck quacked!" He howls while everyone stares. "Me," he keeps going, "I'm in here for soaking my foot in a bucket of bleach. Yep. Kept it in there a bit too long. Skin's eaten away. Want to see? I can take the bandages off for you."

"No!" everyone around him yells.

"Oh, all right. Well, then. How about this one? Man walks into a bar ..."

"What is this guy's problem?" Luke says to Cydni. She only shakes her head.

"Who was that?" Janet asks when she returns, as the guy's being wheeled away.

"Some crazy dude," Luke answers.

"Soaked his foot in bleach," says Cydni.

Janet sits down. "Some guy chooses to hurt himself, and he looks okay. My daughter didn't do anything wrong, and she's ..."

"What did they say, Janet?" Mark asks.

"No news. She's still in surgery."

"What will happen to Mr. Haddings?" Cydni asks.

Janet shrugs, not really focused on her.

"I suppose it depends on Sarah's surgery," Mark answers.

"Will he lose his job though?"

"I'd imagine, if criminal charges are filed. But if not, I suppose he'll keep it, if they declare it an accident."

I swallow the bile back down my throat.

1:34 pm

Mark turns to his wife. "Can I hold on to the scan?"

64

She slips the folded paper from her purse. It's pressed between their palms for a second. Finally, he takes it, opens it up, and studies it. He carefully refolds the scan, sliding it into his breast pocket, behind a pen, which he takes out. "Sarah gave me this pen on Father's Day a few years ago. I think of her each time I use it. Well, at least the first time I use it each day. Sometimes."

The silence is the full-on awkward kind.

He goes on to himself, more than to them. "Did I say good-bye to Sarah this morning? What was she wearing?"

"That shirt she always wears, even though I told her the new one I bought her looked better. And a hoodie," answers Janet.

It was pink.

And that ends that conversation.

2:10 pm

When the volunteer comes over and asks if I need anything, I quickly smile and shake my head so she returns to her desk across the room. With my knee bouncing, I wait, but none of Sarah's family comes around the tank and palm fronds to confront me, so I settle back in the seat.

The people in the room flow in and out like waves. Some roll away quietly, while others roar against the furniture and walls before disappearing down the hall. A few walk in circles like spinning eddies or sit trapped in small tide pools.

I'm a pebble tumbling in the breakwater, waiting for a doctor to fling me onto the sand and tell me Sarah will live, and my future — our futures — are safe.

Cydni comes over to the tank, and I quickly turn my back to her. She mutters to herself, "He messed with her, made her think she was special and that he was all into her, and then he goes and runs her down. Jerk."

No! That's not true! I didn't. What has Sarah believed this whole time, and what has she told Cydni? I didn't lead Sarah on and instead tried to be clear. Pulling in a shaking breath, I whisper, "And I didn't run her down! It was an accident."

I peek and see Cydni return to a seat beside Luke, who says, "I can't keep my mind off it. My mind. My brain. Okay. Don't think of Sares' brain. How it's probably gray. Is it spongy or rubbery? Stop thinking about brains."

Cydni shivers. Chantelle reaches over and pats Luke's back, but he keeps up the monologue.

"Watch the fish instead. Okay. Fish. How big are fish brains? Could you do surgery on a fish's brain? Like that big angelfish? How would it compare to Sares' brain? Stop it! Shut up, brain! Man, I'm sick of this place and waiting! It's been hours now. It's enough to kill a person's brain." He panics and looks to his mom. "Did I jinx Sares?"

"No," Cydni whispers. "This is really hard. It's okay."

Janet ignores Luke. "I should make some calls."

"All right," Mark agrees.

"No, wait. I can't."

"Why?"

"The nurse said you have to go to the top floor of the parking garage to get reception."

Luke leans over. "Signs everywhere say not to use your cell."

"Well," Janet says, "I can't leave this room and miss the doctor. Sarah's going to need me right away."

Mark removes his badge and puts it in his pocket. "You're right. We shouldn't leave."

"Would you like me to go make some calls?" asks Chantelle.

Janet folds her hands. "No. Let's wait. Until we know more. No need to call yet."

Stepping around a baby crawling on the floor, Mark goes over to the bathroom.

"Could Sares die, Mom?" Luke asks.

"That's exactly what I was wondering," Cydni says, swiping at her eyes.

I clutch my cramping stomach.

Janet clicks her purse closed. "We don't know. She could, or, she might—It's a very dangerous surgery. Well, um—" She tucks her hair behind her ear with shaking fingers.

Luke covers her hand, and she leans her head onto his shoulder.

Mark returns, smoothing his hair down. It looks more like he wants to rip it all out.

"Dad?" says Luke.

"When did I stop paying attention to Sarah?" he asks.

No one answers him.

The question niggles into me and morphs. How did Sarah not pay attention and see my car this morning? I grind my heels into the industrial carpet. How is that possible when my headlights were on; can an ounce of blame be moved onto her? Shame heats my face. How did I not pay attention and see her?

2:40 pm

"That's him!"

Startled, I nearly fall off the chair, until I see Luke leap up and point to the surgeon.

"Five hours for an operation is crazy," Luke says to Cydni, who agrees.

67

The surgeon gestures to a small room across the hallway, and Luke follows his folks out. "Be right back," he tells Cydni and Chantelle over his shoulder. They wave him on.

When Cydni goes into the bathroom, I slip out of the waiting area. There's a bulletin board in the hallway, which I act like I'm reading as I listen through the ajar door.

"The surgery has stopped the bleeding." Air gushes out of my chest and flutters the papers tacked to the display. She's alive! She's okay!

"Excellent," Luke says.

"Yes!" Janet exclaims.

The doctor goes on. "However, we won't know for an extended period if Sarah's brain sustained permanent damage. It could take months to identify problems."

I choke. Permanent damage?

"Right now," he says, "we wait to see if the brain returns to its normal shape. Memory, speech, motor, and reasoning skills could all be altered."

It sounds like someone's nails are scratching against a tabletop.

"What can I do?" I whisper.

"What can we do?" Janet asks.

"Sarah's in recovery," the doctor explains. "It will be a few hours before we move her into the ICU. You might think of gathering a few personal effects from home to help make her stay in the hospital more comfortable. She'll be here for several days."

"Yes, we'll do that," says Mark.

"I, I want to see her," Janet begs.

"Yes, I understand. We'll let you know as soon as that is possible. The reception desk will keep you informed." He comes to the doorway.

This is the man who touched Sarah's brain. With his fingers.

"Thank you," Janet whispers. "Thank you for giving my daughter back to me."

The doctor brushes past me. Should I leave now, before possibly getting a chance to talk to Sarah's father and hearing how she comes out of recovery? I can't.

I shrug my jacket closed and return to the waiting room. Cydni is facing away from the entry, so I drop into the same chair as before behind the tank. Sarah's out of surgery, alive, but I need to know more about her recovery.

Luke, Mark, and Janet return and fill in Cydni and Chantelle. I bite at my torn cuticle.

Janet reaches over and pats Luke's back. "Right now, the best thing is for you and your dad to go home and pack a few bags for us. Are you listening? I need your help."

I sit on my hands.

Janet mutters, "Your dad probably wants a break anyway."

"Did you say something, Janet?" Mark's lower jaw is slung to the right.

"Never mind," she says, one brow raised. "And start making phone calls. Get a chain going with church and family. I need you to really help here, Luke."

He and Mark stand. "This is something we can do," he says, throwing his arm around his son. "We'll be back before anyone misses us."

Behind him, Janet rolls her eyes. Can't she give him a break?

"Come on, Luke," Mark says. "You okay to drive yourself home?"

"Yeah."

After Cydni pushes a paper into Luke's hand, she smiles up at him. "My mom and I wrote down some things you might bring back."

Janet intercepts the list. "Let me add a few, too." She scrawls more stuff down on the back of the paper.

"I'm not getting that stuff together. No way," says Luke.

She looks up at him and glares.

"Okay, okay. But I don't know a pad from a tampon, you know." Luke huffs.

"We'll get it figured out," Mark interjects. He takes the list, and the two head out. Luke turns and waves at Cydni, who breaks into a huge grin.

Should I follow now and intercept Mark and Luke? But Sarah's going to need those things, and I don't want to delay them. Maybe I can catch her father alone when he returns?

"How about a cup of coffee?" Chantelle asks Janet.

"Probably don't have time," she answers.

"I'm sure we do," Chantelle urges. "You could check at the desk for when they think Sarah will be moved."

Janet finally relents and walks over to the receptionist. My own stomach gurgles, and I realize I missed lunch.

Janet returns, and Chantelle convinces her she can believe the attendant. There's time to eat. The two women and Cydni finally leave the waiting room. I let out a huge sigh. The little girl across the way looks over at me and hugs her doll closer.

Sarah's survived the surgery. I close my eyes and feel the relief flood me. Before I know it, I'm crying silently.

There's a little tap on my leg. I jump. It's the girl. "It's okay," she says to me and makes her doll pat the back of my hand.

"You're right," I say. "It's okay."

70

Down in the busy cafeteria, I scout the area, but the ladies aren't in sight. I load up my tray with mac and cheese, fries, and a chocolate shake. I pay, then inch into the eating area. It's not that I can't deal with Cydni; I already have, and actually I'd like to set a few things straight. But that's for another time. I just don't want to upset Janet more than she is right now. She needs to focus on Sarah, to be the best help to her.

I spot the trio in the middle of the crowded room at a little table. I edge into a seat behind a nearby pillar. Perfect. I can hear them and even catch their reflection in the dark window. Janet grips her cup, and I shovel into my food.

"We have these huge house payments with the move, what, only three years ago? I mean, we moved so the kids would be in the Covington school district for high school. I can't believe we moved so my daughter could be hit, walking to her bus stop."

"Well, I'm glad you moved near us," says Cydni, but the ladies ignore her.

"And now these hospital bills are going to be astronomical. It's not likely a grad student would carry enough insurance to cover an accident like this," Janet says.

Hey, I've got some coverage. Wait, how much do I have?

Chantelle leans forward. "Don't worry about the money, or work at the office, or even pressing charges right now. You need all your energy focused on Sarah. She's what's important."

Charges? The cold milkshake burns my throat.

Janet sips her drink. "You are right," she says. "Thanks for being a sounding board, Chantelle."

"It's the least I can do," she says.

71

After a moment, Janet continues. "It's like everything shifts in a tragedy. As if someone grips your chin and jerks it where you weren't looking a moment before. The sight is horrid, but you know for certain all your energy has to go into that one place. Oh, shoot. I've spilled my coffee."

"Wait here. I'll get a few napkins." Chantelle crosses the room.

Janet doesn't miss a beat. "Some teacher—"

"Yeah, I know, Mrs. McCormick," Cydni says. "It was Mr. Haddings."

This gets repeated a couple more times before Chantelle returns.

"He hit my daughter with his car!" says Janet.

"Yes, he did, Janet," Chantelle answers.

All of a sudden, my food slugs my stomach. I swallow, ignoring it, eating one fry after another, cramming the greasy pile into my mouth.

"He hit her with his car!"

I belch into my napkin.

CHAPTER 16

Sarah

<u>5:05 pm</u>

Beep.
   Beep.
   Beeeeep.
   Jostle.
   So ... chilled.
   Warm air
   puffs.
   My head aches. Deeply raw.
   Sleep ... ing.

CHAPTER 17

Haddings

6:20 pm

I drop onto the bench outside the children's ICU waiting room. Cydni's, her mom's, and Janet's voices carry from behind the double doors. When the nurse said Sarah was being moved out of recovery, I headed up here a few minutes after them. The staff has to take her through this hall to get into the ward, I think, so maybe I can see her.

Wait—why are they placing her in a children's ward?

I eventually discover the answer by overhearing Janet: there's a bed available in children's, and Sarah will get closer attention here than she would in the adult ward.

"She's not a child though," Cydni responds.

Exactly. In the fall, Sarah will be starting college. Before class a few weeks ago, she mentioned she had her choices narrowed

74

down to Mills or UW. It's hard to imagine being in school with her in Seattle; it's all too strange. I shiver. Right now, I don't even know if she can finish high school.

"Sarah's technically an adult, since she turned eighteen last month," Cydni says.

"She'll always be my child," Janet answers.

A couple hurries past me through the doors. The nearly empty waiting room is full of little furniture alongside adult-size chairs and tables. I glimpse images of flowers and happy children on the walls before the doors swing shut again.

"Look, out this window you can see a camera crew is down there," says Chantelle.

Are they reporting my accident? What I did? I draw my feet up onto the bench and hide my face against my knees. Please, please, no.

"I'll check the TV," Cydni says. There's the sound of channel surfing, tumbling words, jingles, sports updates.

"Why don't you two go on home now? Get some dinner," Janet suggests. "Mark and Luke will be back soon. You don't need to stay. It's getting late. I've got everything under control."

I drop my feet to the floor, but Chantelle answers immediately. "We're not going anywhere right now. We want to see Sarah, and we are not leaving you alone."

"I'm okay," she argues.

The TV rants, one station, then the next.

"Well," Janet eventually says. "Whatever you feel you need to do is fine. I'm not going to spend my energy arguing with you about it."

"There! Look!" says Cydni.

"Early this morning in Covington," the newscaster relays, "a teen walking to her bus stop was hit by a car in a crosswalk. The driver was not detained, although charges are pending."

My heart skips out of beat.

"Do you have an update, Julie?"

"The eighteen-year-old girl, a student at Kentlake High School, remains in critical condition. There is no further information at this time."

The TV goes mute. "How weird was that?" Cydni says. "I mean, like, they could have interviewed me, you know, since I saw the whole thing happen. I would have talked to them, then everyone would have seen me on TV—not that that's important or anything. It's Sarah we are thinking about," she concludes with a hushed voice.

"Pending charges" rattles my mind. Not homicide. Not manslaughter, but still, some sort of legal repercussion. I need a lawyer ASAP.

The staff elevator at the end of the hall dings. I hold my breath. After the wide door opens, a body is rolled out. Two attendants block my view as they push the person closer. The male stops right in front of me. Is it Sarah? I clutch the front of the bench. The woman nudges the gurney through the waiting room doors.

"I have to see," I plead, standing and peeking into the room.

Janet lumbers to the bed, and the attendants slow for a moment. "Sarah?" she whispers, and leans over. "Oh, Sarah!"

I stand on my toes, straining for a glimpse.

"Is she dead?" Cydni's shrill voice rises. "Is my friend dead?" The male attendant pulls her aside and talks quietly to her. Chantelle is bawling her head off.

The woman attendant turns to Janet. "Ma'am, we're taking Sarah into ICU, and then a nurse will come get you. We want to get her cleaned up and comfortable." She tries to roll the gurney forward.

"Let me take care of her," Janet demands. "I'll clean her up. I'll take care of my daughter now."

"No, ma'am. That's our job," the attendant says.

The male props Cydni in a chair. "There, now." He turns to Sarah's mom and grasps her arms. He walks her a step back from the gurney. "The sooner we go and do our work, the sooner we can come and get you. It will only be a few minutes. Okay?"

Janet tries to reach around him, but he holds her back as the female attendant punches a code into a keypad. Quickly, they push Sarah through the ICU doors, which shut behind them.

Janet turns to Chantelle. "Don't say anything!" she yells. "She looks beautiful! My daughter is still beautiful! Don't you say anything otherwise! She — is — beautiful!"

Chantelle runs off to the bathroom, where her crying only echoes louder. Janet slams her hands against the locked doors that lead into ICU. "She is beautiful!" she wails to no one.

"Excuse me."

I turn and come face to face with the surgeon. "Oh, I'm sorry." I step behind the door and open it for him. He strides across the room while I open the door a smidge wider to watch.

"Mrs. McCormick," he says, breaking the insane spell she's in. She wipes her eyes with the back of her wrist and hurries to his side.

"The follow-up CAT scan confirms the surgery's effort."

"Effort?" Chantelle asks, coming out of the bathroom.

"The scan," the doctor continues, "shows no further bleeding. The titanium plate screwed onto the skull is holding the pieces in place."

"Screwed?" asks Janet.

"Yes, screwed onto her skull."

"Will she start bleeding again?" Cydni asks, getting up from the chair.

"No. Neurological damage is the concern now."

"But she's okay?" Cydni says. "She's not dead or anything—"

The doctor smiles. "She's sedated." He hands Janet a piece of paper.

"The blood pool is gone," she says, clutching the neck of her shirt closed.

"Yes, and the brain is beginning to regain its shape," the surgeon answers. "We'll start testing very soon for further damage; although, as I said earlier, it will take months to determine her full state. I'll go and examine her now. It won't be long, though, before they take you to her."

Janet reaches out and squeezes his thin hand. "I need to see Sarah now. I need to take care of her."

"Yes, Mrs. McCormick. You'll be taken inside in a few moments." He slips from her grasp, punches in the code, and disappears inside the unit.

Janet and Chantelle embrace and begin rehashing everything the surgeon said.

That's it. I can't stand it. I'm going to go in and introduce myself and get this over with. I'll weather their reaction; I just have to get inside and see Sarah myself—if only her mother will allow it. Maybe I can be of help right now. I step into the room.

Cydni looks up, and we stare at each other, still as statues. "No," she mouths, rushing at me, her curls wired in fury all over her head like Medusa's snakes. She shoves me into the hall, and the door clunks closed behind us.

"What are you doing?" she yells in a whisper.

I step back, trying to pull an answer up from my blank mind.

She elbows me toward the elevator, and I stumble as she herds me to the doors and crams the down button. "What are you doing here?" she spits into my face.

"I had to know."

"Had to know what?"

"I had to know she's all right," I say.

She glances over her shoulder. "All right? If Sarah's all right? Are you kidding me? Didn't you see—" She shakes her head. "What if Mrs. McCormick sees you? You are such a selfish jerk! You're the last person she's going to want to see right now. She's nearly losing it already without meeting you."

"No, no. That's why I didn't intrude. I was only waiting nearby—but now I thought Sarah's mother might want an explanation, or to, I don't know, have the opportunity to vent at me. I, I want to take responsibility for—"

"You creep! You're a total stalker. What is wrong with you? No one wants you here."

When the elevator dings, Cydni reaches out and holds the door of the empty car open. "So, did you see, see what you did? How 'all right' Sarah is, because of you? You made my friend look like a freaking Frankenstein, some Tim Burton character, you idiot. She's got a plate screwed into her head. Screwed!" She jabs me with her finger.

"But, her mother said, she said she's still beautiful."

"She's in shock! It's total denial, obviously." She rolls her eyes. "You're so stupid."

Squeezing by into the elevator, I absorb the hate streaming

out of her. She flings her hair off her face. "It makes me sick to look at you."

"I'm going," I say. "You're right. I shouldn't be here. I'm sorry, so sorry."

"Good, go! Get out"—she crosses her arms—"because I can take care of Sarah. She for sure doesn't need you. She never did. She needs me. Get out of here!"

The doors close, and my knees buckle while the elevator descends. My whole body's shaking. The car stops, and I manage to pull myself upright. A tall guy in a cowboy hat with a bunch of flowers and a giant grin and an old woman shuffling with her oxygen tank join me.

Grasping for peace, I recall Sarah's voice, not Cydni's, from class when she recited one of the poems she absolutely loved. The Shoha Japanese haiku:

> Rainfall in April
> tears from our weeping willow
> petals from our plum

"It's beautiful," she said, looking up at me with wide eyes, seemingly oblivious to the room of kids around her. "I love haikus."

The elevator slows, and the doors open again to a man in a wheelchair who rolls in beside me. He's hooked up to an IV, with bolts coming out of his knee and bandages wrapped around his neck. There's a smell seeping from him that fills the car.

The last bit of energy I had slides down my legs faster than the elevator drops. Holding my breath, I barely can stay upright in the corner until we reach the lobby. I stumble out, right behind the poor wheelchair guy. He turns the corner and heads the opposite direction while I make it across the main lobby and fall into a maroon chair. The high ceiling towers above me in looming judgment. I drop my head in my hands, taking deep, slow breaths, waiting for my stomach to settle.

"She's in children's ICU, Dad. Come on, I have to see what she looks like." It's Luke.

"Let's go then," Mark answers, jostling a couple overnight bags. The two of them disappear across the shiny white floor before I can muster the strength to catch them. Anyway, Cydni's probably right. I have no right to be here.

I sit back, reliving her insults and hatred, and wipe the tears off until they abate. No one is going to care if I'm sorry or not, and apparently there's nothing I can do for Sarah. I rub the back of my neck, and the gift kiosk catches my eye.

Walking over, I stop before the bears and candy overflowing the stand. I point to the dozen red roses in the mini refrigerator, sitting all alone. "Can these be delivered to Sarah McCormick in children's ICU?"

"No, but we can keep the order until she's moved into a room. Would you like that?" the cashier asks, her arched brows raised.

"Yes, that would be great."

"All right then, and here's a card to sign."

"No, thanks. I'll skip the card."

She puts it back and processes the sale, humming under her breath.

I punch my pin into the machine. My fingers tap on the counter as I shift from one foot to the other. "Thanks." I take the receipt and simply walk away. The best I can do is leave them all alone.

CHAPTER 18

Sarah

8:23 pm

"Haddings," I murmur.

"What did she say?"

I try to open my eyes. "Mom?" I croak. Focus. Try to focus.

There. There she ... is. Her face is so close, she has four eyes. She draws back with a huge smile. "Mom, they said—I was going—to have—a funny haircut."

She tucks her hair behind her ear. "Yes, it's pretty silly, sweetheart, but you are still beautiful. Everything is fine now. You rest."

My eyes slip closed.

"Are you okay, Luke?" Dad asks.

"Someone call the nurse," Mom cries. "Dottie! Nurse Dottie. She just spoke! She woke for a moment, and my baby spoke!"

Shhh! Please, oh, please. My head. Be quiet. I have to sleep and get away from this pain, pain, pain. I never ever want to wake again.

But they don't shut up. They—keep—talking.

"Now see there? Didn't I tell you?" says an unfamiliar voice.

"Doesn't she look good, Luke?" Mom whispers.

"Are you kidding, Mom?" he says. "This is like a horror film."

"Luke!"

"Mom, look at all these tubes and the blood. Her hair!"

Maybe a chair is knocked over? I drift away, far away.

9:16 pm

I return at some point.

"Now, don't you worry," the unknown voice says again. "And don't spend an ounce of worry on her hair, Janet."

"Are you sure, Dottie?" asks Dad.

"Yes. It will grow back beautifully. Let me check her vitals again. Her oxygen."

Who are they talking about? Is it me? My hair?

There's a pinch on my finger. A prod. A poke. I try to open my eyes again, but I can't.

"Can't they cover up the grossness?" asks Luke.

"Everything will heal better exposed to the air," Dottie answers.

"Well, what's that lump thing stuffed under her scalp?"

"Drainage."

"Man, I can't believe that guy did this to her, Dad. I mean, compare this to her senior photos. Seriously? I want to cream him with my truck, you know?"

"Let's focus on the positive," Dottie says.

83

"That's right," Mom answers. "The surgeon said we'll be the signal for how Sarah should react."

It is about me. This is something about me. There's a cool kiss against my left cheek.

"That gives me the creeps you can do that, Mom."

"Luke!"

I float away.

10:04 pm

I come back to Luke whispering. "I can't believe I couldn't wait to see her! I just wanted to be sure she didn't look like a freak, but she does! Look how huge her head is. Don't you think her skin's actually green? And those black stitches and red ones clumped with brown blood chunks. Oh, man. She looks like death. A zombie, right?"

"Shhhhhh," is the only reply. Who? Who was he talking to? Who was he talking about now? It sounded horrible.

"We all agree? We will not tell her who the driver was," says Mom.

"That's right. It will only upset her more," someone else says.

"But maybe she needs to know."

Was that Cydni?

"No!" several people say. I glide off before I can even try to ask what they are talking about.

10:32 pm

"This is her senior year, for crying out loud! What? She's supposed to go to school like this? Like some monster? Who would ever ask to take her to prom?" spews Luke.

"She's still beautiful!" Mom argues.

"Whatever, Mom. Just keep denying this really happened."

"Enough, Luke," says Dad. "Did you see that poor moaning child a few doors down? He was covered in bandages from the waist up. Let's all take the time to be thankful Sarah is okay."

I'm okay! Isn't that what he said? So, why can't I wake up? What is wrong with me?

He goes on. "There's so much pain in this ward. So much to pray for."

Are you praying for me, Daddy?

"Sares, I'm here, too."

"Cydni?" My eyes flutter. It is Cydni. She's sitting next to me on this bed, wherever that is.

"Did you hear that?" asks my mom.

"She recognized me! Me, her best friend who is going to help her get better. I promise, Sares!"

I try my hardest to hold on, but I lose my grip and fall asleep.

CHAPTER 19

Haddings

<u>10:35 pm</u>

Alone in my tiny flat, I'm grateful I don't have a roommate I'd have to shrug off right now. It took long enough to answer my friends' texts and convince them not to come over. No, I don't want any company tonight.

Having parked under a streetlight, I was able to see to scrub my car seat clean. I ran my hand over the small dents in the grill and across the hood. I didn't look at the car damage at the hospital because I was focused on finding Sarah, I guess. But the dings are irrefutable proof of what I did.

Finally, I plodded back up to my flat. I showered and changed, balled my dirty clothes into the hamper, and folded my leather jacket to hide the blood stains. Maybe the cleaners can get everything out.

Now, I set my empty Mac & Jack's bottle on the cement floor. My round paper light glows above me like an eyeball while I sit beneath it, huddled in the center of my bed.

I underline the lawyer's number my prof gave me and flip my notebook closed. What a relief he's excused me from classes and papers for a couple days.

Bunching a pillow in my lap, I dial up my folks, despite the time difference in Boulder. My ear rings through my mother's rant. "I understand having an accident, Jake. Anyone can have an accident, and we can hope the girl is going to be okay, but why, why didn't you carry a better policy on your car?"

"I thought that was enough, Mom."

"Do you realize we are going to have to take a second mortgage for the hospital bills alone? Do you know the strain that will put your father under?"

"No, no," I argue. "It's my responsibility. I'm going to figure it out."

"Just like your school loans are your responsibility, and we've ended up helping how many times?"

"Once, Mom. Okay, maybe twice, I couldn't make the payment. But the bill is suspended now since I'm back in school."

"I know that, Jake," she snips. "That's not the point."

Silence.

"Let's think a minute." She takes a deep breath. "Okay. Is it possible … I mean, I can tell you, over the years I've had cases like this at the shelter—just last week a young man threw himself in front of a bus out of desperation. You say this girl came out of nowhere. Is there any chance she intentionally stepped in front of your car?"

"What? What are you saying, Mom?"

87

"Just that there'd be no culpability on your part, Jake, if this was a cry for help, an attempted teen suicide."

"No, Mom. No, she wouldn't do that. She's very stable." She'd never try to kill herself.

I pick at the Tom Petty sticker on the back of my journal. Yeah, I read my poem to the class, but my rejection wouldn't have incited Sarah to step out in front of a car. Even if she believed what Cydni said earlier—that I led her on—it's too ridiculous.

"I'm only suggesting that be explored," Mom repeats. "It would explain things. Teen suicide rates are higher—"

"Can I talk to Dad, Mom?"

My father is quiet when he takes the phone. The truckload of disappointed silence is worse than Mom's reaction.

"Please don't pull overtime yet, Dad. I want to try to work this out."

"That's good to hear, but this will be enormous, Jake. We'll wait and see." Mom interrupts in the background. "No, I don't think we should fly out, Margery. We need to save that money." He comes back to me. "Have you been to the hospital, Jake?"

"Um, yeah."

"And did you see the parents?"

"I saw them, but they didn't—no. I really didn't think they'd want to see me."

There's a long pause. "Well, think about it. Think about what the right thing to do is. In the meantime, stay focused, and stay in class." Dad clears his throat. "Neither your mom nor I would want you to give up on your degree."

I swallow. "Have to go, Dad."

I shove my cell aside and crawl under the covers with my shame.

"Yzma," I call my Siamese cat, but she doesn't come. In fact, she walks right out of the room, her tail flicking side to side.

I open my journal to the poem I wrote and read in front of the class.

Never

Never
can it be.
Never was it
meant to be.
Never will it
ever be.
You
and
me,
even when
you say,
Just wait;
we'll see.

Never,
ever,
my friend.

I followed it up with Shiki's work:

Tranquility:
Walking alone,
Happy alone.

CHAPTER 20

Sarah

I surface again, but I can't move, even an eyelid. I know more though. I remember. I was walking to school ...

That car didn't stop. The headlights veer close. I slam onto the hood and fly through the rain.

A whimper cuts past my dry throat and out my puffy lips.

"Oh, hand me a tissue!" Someone dabs my cheeks. "You're okay, sweetheart," says Mom.

I roll my head away from her hand. Pain shoots out my forehead, but I try to focus through it, hold on even if I can't open my eyes. I had surgery, brain surgery! Wait, wait. I was in an ambulance, and then I flew in a helicopter. They said I was going to have a funny haircut, and I was worried I was going to

90

die. I didn't. I didn't die. I'm still here! The thought patters like soft, warm rain all over my skin.

I flinch when the pain circles back around and snaps me. It slowly disappears in the thickness around my body. I pant, coming out of the agony.

There's something stuck in my nose. I raise my hand to wipe it away but get tangled in tubing.

"Lie still, sweetie," Mom whispers into my ear.

Sniveling, I try to wipe my nose with my shoulder.

"It's just oxygen, Sarah. It's helping you," says Dad.

I start falling asleep in the middle of their excited chatter.

"She moved her hand, her whole arm!"

"I saw her foot move."

"And her head. She turned it! Did you see that?"

Shhhhhhhh, please.

10:51 pm

Coming back, I enter the stream of an argument.

"Now, Luke?" Mom asks.

"Yeah. I mean, it's late, and I have school tomorrow. So, there's her stuff in the corner. I dug through her trashed room, Mom. At least give me credit for getting everything from the list for her."

He went through my things?

"You did a good job, Luke," says Dad.

"Oh, and here's her blanket thingy."

My baby blanket?

"Oh, she can't have that right now," someone says.

"You think, Chantelle?"

"I'm sure it's not clean enough."

But I want it. Can't someone ask me?

"I'll take it," says Dad softly.

"Yeah. So I, you know, need to get out of here," Luke says. "What, Mom? Look. I can't take this. She looks like a freak."

What? What does he mean?

"Luke!"

"I'm keeping it real, okay? Sarah's so out of it, she's not hearing us."

Yes, I am!

"Don't you say such things, Luke! Sarah can hear you." Someone rests their hand on mine. I flinch from the pain.

"So, do you need a ride, Cydni? I can take you home if your mom wants to stay longer."

"Um. Well, I guess, I want to — stay."

Dad coughs. "All right, son. You go do what you need to."

"Oh, great," Mom cuts in. "Go ahead and enable him, Mark!"

"Not now, Janet. Drive carefully, Luke." Keys rattle.

"Yeah, yeah, I will." There's a shuffled walking. "But when Sares really wakes up, um, tell her I was here, if she doesn't remember, and tell her that, you know, I love her and stuff."

Really? Did he just say that out loud?

"You can tell her, Luke," says Mom, "when you come back tomorrow."

11:11 pm

I think I must have fallen asleep again, because now's there laughter.

92

"Why, Mark, did you bring me six bras?" There's a burst of snickering. "You think I needed this black lacy one particularly? What were you thinking this time?"

"Well, I thought you needed one per day. No one has said how long they'll keep Sarah. Don't you need a bra a day?"

"And what did you bring for yourself?" A zipper is opened. "Yes, Mark. You are going to need what, oh, seven books to read?"

"It's okay, Mr. McCormick," Cydni says. "That looks like a good book. We're studying the Oregon Trail in AP American History. I bet when Sarah's feeling better, you could read some to her."

I do like the Oregon Trail.

"I think so, too," he says. "But are six bras over the top, really?"

"Yeah."

I finally open my eyes, and everything clears. Mom is holding a pile of bras. Dad's holding a book. Everyone is giggling.

"What's so funny?" I ask in a hoarse, thick voice.

"She's awake!" They swarm the bed, but no one ever thinks to say what they were laughing at.

CHAPTER 21

Haddings

11:54 pm

Not able to sleep, I'm hoping another shower settles me down. I stand in the stall as the water thrums my back. "I am not going back to the hospital." My dad doesn't understand. Even Cydni knows that's the last thing I should do.

With a fist on either side of the showerhead, I tilt my head and open my mouth. "No!" gurgles up through the water. I spit and lean my forehead against the wall.

I'm going to go back to bed, where I'll finally be able to sleep and escape.

The spigot drips when I turn it off. *Go, go, go,* it taps.

CHAPTER 22

Sarah

12:14 am

Apparently, it's the middle of the night, or morning, but they are still going to keep asking me this stuff. Yes, I know who each of them is. I wiggle my toes and fingers. With each little accomplishment, there's a collective celebration, as if I've actually accomplished something amazing. Cydni can't stop beaming at me. "I'm here for you," she keeps saying, hovering on the stool beside me. "Right here."

"Thanks," I whisper. She's such a good friend.

"Please, Mom," I beg, trying to keep my eyes open. "Let Cydni tell me what happened. It will help me ... clear my mind and remember. Everything is blurry."

"I don't think it's a good idea right now. So soon," my mother answers.

95

"Really, Mom." I try to smile, wondering if I managed to. "It will help."

"Do you think it will?" Cydni's mom asks my parents.

"Maybe," says Dad. He gives a nod to Cydni.

Mom scowls then turns her back to us and stares out the night-filled window.

Cydni starts, and I try to focus on her face. "So, you were under the streetlight, and then you stepped into the crosswalk."

"Go on," I say, as she blurs in my tears.

"Well, there was a blue car," she says, "coasting down the big hill."

"Uh huh."

"A Mustang," Chantelle adds. She scoots her chair closer to the bed.

"A what?"

"A blue Mustang, Sarah." Cydni pauses a second. "What happened was, you came across the street, but then you needed to go back for something you dropped."

"Maybe so?" I try to remember.

"I offered to get it, but you said no. Then I was checking my phone. When I looked up and saw the car not even slowing down, I yelled. You stood up but didn't have a chance to get out of the way. You didn't have a chance."

I nod and jerk in shallow breaths.

"And then the car hit you." She sits on the edge of the bed. "The blue Mustang," she says slowly, a knowing look on her face.

I can only stare at her until she goes on. "When he hit you, all your stuff went everywhere. Your shoes, even one of your socks ended up in a bush. Maybe your messenger bag took a lot of the impact, before it was ripped apart?"

96

"It's possible." says Dad, "Still, the doctor said the bruises on your legs will be sore for a good while."

The blanket is too heavy to move, so I can't check my aching legs.

Cydni keeps going. "So yeah, then you were bashed up onto the guy's hood, all twisted, and your notebooks and papers went everywhere while you were thrown straight past me. I don't know, twenty-five feet or something? When you hit the road, it cracked your skull right open, and you skidded pretty far."

I gasp, and then I'm blubbering like a baby.

"Cydni, that's enough," says Chantelle.

Glowering at my friend, Mom pushes past her to get to my side. "Was all that really necessary?"

Cydni stands, tears in her eyes.

"Her heart rate's shot up," says Dad on my other side.

"Sweetheart, it's okay." Mom pets my arm, strokes my shoulder.

I shrink from her excruciating touch. "That hurts. Stop. Stop it, Mom!"

She pulls away as a nurse barges into the room and flies over all the machines. She increases one of the IV drips. "There's some more morphine, dear," she says to me, dabbing my cheeks with a square piece of gauze.

An oozing calmness flows all around inside my body. I let out a big sigh.

The nurse turns to everyone with a patronizing smile. "Let's do our best not to upset the patient."

"I'm sorry," Cydni whispers. "I'm sorry," she mouths to me again.

"It's ... okay," I slur.

The nurse leaves, and I manage to ask, "It was a man?"

Cydni nods. "Yep. You could say that."

"Just some man," Mom repeats through tight lips.

"It was an accident," my dad says.

I reach up, touch my cheek, and find it all goopy, but my mom immediately takes my palm and lowers it. "You don't want to touch your face, Sarah."

My arms go limp as the drugs take over completely.

Through the covers, Dad squeezes my toes. "I don't want you to waste your strength on hostility toward the driver, Sarah. All that matters, in this moment, is that my baby girl is alive. Do you hear me, Sarah?"

I close my eyes and sniffle. "I'm glad you are here, Daddy."

"Me, too, baby girl. You've got my full attention from here on out. Okay?"

I lift my heavy eyelids. "Thanks." I think I'm going to need it.

From then on, it's pretty quiet. Maybe everyone is afraid to say anything else that might upset me? But what more could there be? Some man ran me down. He hit me. I keep my eyes closed, while I drift.

Eventually, Cydni's mom says, "We should probably go. You'll rest better, Sarah, without us leaning over you."

I look at her and smile, "'kay."

"But I don't want to leave Sarah, Mom," Cydni says, coming to my bedside.

"I don't want you to leave," I agree.

She tilts her head. "I want to see them get all these creepo machines off."

"These machines are each doing something very important, Cydni." Mom adjusts the tube on my right hand.

"Right," Cydni says. "I guess so. Well, I'll come tomorrow after school. How's that?"

"Promise?" I ask.

"Yep." Cydni weaves her arms around and under the wires and tubes. She reaches me below the maze and gives me the gentlest hug. I don't have any strength to return it.

"Be careful there," says Mom.

"They are fine," Dad counters.

"I can't believe he did this," Cydni whispers.

"I know," I answer. "Thanks for being here with me." I start crying again. "You are my best friend from forever."

"From forever to forever. I'll be back," she says, pulling away.

Mom wipes the snot leaking out of me around the nose piece. She dabs my eyes.

"So, um." They all wait for me to go on. "Did anyone … find my flute?" I ask and hiccup. The silence is thick, like we are suffocating in Jell-O. They look at each other and dart their eyes from mine.

"What flute, honey?" asks Mom.

"Mine." I close my eyes and then slowly open them again. "The one you bought me. You know, on eBay." I wipe my nose on the sheet this time.

My mother bites her ragged lip.

Cydni pats my foot through the blanket. "Oh, you're a little confused, Sarah. Remember? You don't play flute. You don't own one, but Dineva just got her open-hole flute. You must be thinking of Dineva's."

I squeeze my eyes shut. What? What does she mean? When I look at everyone again, more tears tip out. "Oh, riiiight," I say. "Dineva's."

Dad fishes in his bag. Mom tucks my blanket more tightly at the foot of the bed.

"Well, then," Chantelle says. "We'll be going."

"Bye," Cydni calls from the door.

"Come back," I mouth.

"I will," she answers.

"Let me walk you to the elevator," says Dad. The door closes behind him.

My breath jags into my lungs in chunks. "Wasn't Luke here, Mom? I heard him, didn't I?"

She turns and studies one of the monitors. "He was here, but he had to get home. He said—to tell you he loves you."

Right. I remember. But couldn't he have stuck it out a little longer? Doesn't he love me that much?

"And the driver hasn't been—"

"No, no." She grimaces.

Of course the driver wouldn't come. "I do remember Luke being here," I say. My voice sounds weak and pathetic, as drained as everyone's faces looked when I mentioned my flute. Maybe they're wrong. Because I remember it, the blue velvet lining the box.

A chill crackles my back. Wait. I'm in speech and debate. It's the same time as marching band after school, isn't it? Why would I have a flute when I'm in debate?

I pick at a loose thread on the sheet. Forget it. Forget it for now. And forget Luke not staying longer.

"Luke was so upset for you. I lost count of how many times he threw up."

"Ew."

"He does care, Sarah."

"Sure." I gently roll my head, but there's no glimpse of Dad yet. My breathing starts to go spastic again, and I fight to calm it. The skin on my forehead pulls tight like when I was little and Mom tugged my ponytails up high. I carefully roll my head back and go to feel my face.

Mom turns and quickly pulls my hand down. "Don't touch," she says.

"Mom." I sigh with as much exasperation as I can gather. "I think I can touch my own face."

"No, we can't risk infection."

I roll my aching eyes. Whatever. I'll fight with her later. "So what is all this?"

She points to different wires. "Blood pressure, oxygen, IVs. The circles are from EKGs. Let's see … pulse, drain tube, and catheter."

"Ugh. That's what hurts down there."

"The nurse said the catheter will probably come out tomorrow."

My blush burns up into what must be tight stitches.

"Oh, and compression boots on your legs. Do you feel them?"

"Yeah." Every now and then it feels like big socks squeeze my calves. "That's so weird."

"Take a sip." Mom holds the water cup and straw, and I pull in the coolness. My mouth is coated with paste, or I would have said no.

"That's good," she says. She reaches over and rubs some lotion into my hands around the tape and wires. Deep anxiety nests between her brows.

"Thanks." I hold up my finger with the clip squeezing it. The monitor glows red on the end. "E.T. phone home," I say, like everyone else who's ever had to wear one of these things. But it makes my mom smile. "I want to sleep, Mommy." Did I just call her Mommy? I'm so obviously drugged.

She rubs the excess lotion into her own hands. "You do that, Sarah. I'll be right here."

Flute music vibrates my cracked skull as the car approaches again. Dad's words wash over me. Don't waste any energy on the driver. With the morphine, I don't know if I'm hearing him repeat himself or I'm imagining him.

"She's alive. She's speaking. She's likely not disfigured permanently. There may not be lasting brain damage. There's so very much to be thankful for, Janet."

Mom whispers, "But she thinks she plays the flute."

There's a long quiet, and then someone says, "It's as if every stitch pokes in and out of my own heart."

And then I hear crying. Is it Mom? Dad? For all I know, it could be me.

2:30 am

I wake a lot less groggy when the neurologist arrives to check my reflexes. His little goatee twitches as he tests and records everything.

The examination shows my legs and arms have good movement and feeling. I don't have to wear the compression sock things anymore. "So I can walk and stuff, right?" I ask through clenched teeth, riding the pain from all the movement.

"Yes. Yes, you can."

"Thought so." I let out a jerky sigh.

"When the anesthetic wears off, you'll need further painkillers though. Just be sure to ask," the doctor says.

"She will," my mom answers.

"Mom, he was talking to me."

"Even your irritation sounds wonderful to me, Sarah." Mom grins like a loon. She turns and talks under her breath to Dad. "She was just confused for a second about the flute. I'm going to still ask though ..."

"Okay," says the doctor. "Try to sleep, despite the nurses checking on you frequently. Any questions?"

A thousand cluster behind my lips, but I can't grab hold of any. Before either of my folks can ask a single thing themselves, the neurologist excuses himself. "I'm being called." He exits right away.

"There was one thing—" Mom says too late.

Dad quickly tries to counter her frustration. "No worries. We'll have plenty of opportunities to get answers. Since he okayed clear liquids for Sarah, why don't I head down to the nurses' station to see if I can score a Popsicle? I saw they keep a stash in the fridge." He winks at me. "Be back in a sec."

While we wait for Dad, Mom rinses my bloody washcloth in the sink beside my bed. The red swirls in circles before slipping down the drain. I mutter aloud by accident, "I wonder what it would be like to see the driver? He's not in jail, right?"

"No, he's not at this point, but are you saying, Sarah, that you would want to see him?"

"No. No, I mean, how could he hit me, right? I don't know what I'd do if he came through the door right now. Cry or scream, but maybe I'd like the opportunity, you know? It's what my mind keeps turning back to ... the missing piece, I guess."

"Well, let's focus on your healing instead," she says and wrings the cloth super hard before hanging it on the side of the sink.

"Okay, but it was an accident. Right, Mom? There's no way that man meant to hurt me, is there?" I whisper.

Mom sits on the tippy edge of my bed and traces the IV tube. "Of course he'd never mean it intentionally, Sarah, but he did hit you. I, personally, will never be able to forgive him."

"Right." I clasp my hands.

"One missing piece that you can control, honey, is to see yourself. Would that help you process things? I have a hand mir—"

"No!" I snap. I definitely don't. The creeps crawl over my skin.

"Oh, all right. I'm sorry; that's fine. It was just a thought." She gets up and tidies the room.

I feel bad for the people who have already had to look at me. Still, I'd rather not know what they've been looking at yet. At least Haddings won't see me like this. It was humiliating enough to listen to his stupid poem last class, and that Shiki one about being alone. How horrible to think of him seeing me now, whatever I look like. Goopy is all I know.

I lift my face. Well, it's not like Haddings would come here, and who knows when I'll make it back to school—if I make it back. To my school. Which is called ... uh. Its name is ... Well, it will come to me. I'm for sure not asking and freaking out Mom again. Stuff like that slips everyone's mind, right?

Wait! My poem for Haddings, the one to counter his. It's out there somewhere. Is it still in my pocket? If anyone finds it, it could be damaging to both of us. I'm so stupid!

And, and that's why I darted back into the street. I ran for the stupid poem. A chill stipples my skin. Is it my fault I got hit?

I blink slowly, and my panic settles. No. No, it's not my fault. There's no way, because how could the driver have not seen me in the crosswalk, under a streetlight? Oh, and I even motioned for him to wait. I totally remember that.

"Um, Mom, where are my clothes from the accident?"

"I don't know, honey. Don't worry about them. We'll replace everything," she says as a nurse enters the room.

"Look'a here." It's the nurse with the accent. Dottie, maybe? She's carrying an enormous vase of red roses. I inhale quickly at the surprise and beautiful scent. "There's not a card anywhere to be seen," she says and stops to smell the blooms. "Now, I don't know how this happened, because flowers aren't allowed in ICU, but these were delivered, and I couldn't bear to send them back. I'll keep them in the nurses' break room until you are relocated, but I thought you'd like to see them for just a sec."

"Thank you," I answer.

Mom steps over and breathes in the scent. "Maybe they're from the gals at work? Or from your dad's office?"

"Maybe a secret admirer?" Dottie teases and moves the IV stand closer to my bed. She holds the bouquet to my nose.

"So beautiful," I say.

She winks. "I'll have them for you later, okay?"

I nod, and she carries out the vase. A flush lingers on my face. Red roses ... from Haddings? Did he hear about the accident? The roses are like the poem by Robert Burns, which I memorized straightaway after he quoted it.

A Red, Red Rose

O my luve's like a red, red rose
That's newly sprung in June;
O my luve's like a melodie
That's sweetly play'd in tune.

As fair art thou, my bonnie lass,
So deep in luve am I;
And I will luve thee still, my Dear,
Till a' the seas gang dry.

Till a' the seas gang dry, my Dear,
And the rocks melt wi' the sun:
I will luve thee still, my Dear,
While the sands o' life shall run.

And fare thee weel, my only Luve!
And fare thee weel a while!
And I will come again, my Luve,
Tho' it were ten thousand mile!

After he read it, Cydni and I fought for days over whether it was a secret message. I drove her crazy bringing it up. At the time, I totally believed Haddings was declaring his love to me. Cydni said the "Never" poem proved the Burns poem was a fluke; he wasn't ever really into me. So, why would he send red roses now?

No one would describe me as "fair" after this accident. A lump sits in my throat.

The rich scent lingers. Hold on a second. Is he saying he didn't mean his stupid poem after all? Did he hear I was hit and come to his senses or something?

"My luve?" I whisper. "Could he care?"

"What, dear?" asks Mom.

"Nothing." Crushing grief swoops onto my chest and stabs the chirp of hope before it can hatch. It's too late, with my bashed face and cracked head, and who knows about my brains, remembering stuff that didn't ever happen, not remembering other things I should. Maybe something with Haddings was actually possible before, but now it's too late. I measure my breath to get it under control, but it's so, so hard when I'm crying.

Mom dabs my eyes. "You okay?"

I shake my head and look away. It's too late for me and him.

"Can I get you something, sweetie?"

"Nothing," I whisper.

When Dad saunters into the room with a teddy bear under his arm, Mom instantly criticizes him. "I thought you were looking for a Popsicle."

"There was no one at the desk, so I jotted downstairs and found this little shop still open. No Popsicle, but they had this for you, Sarah."

I reach out and take the stuffed animal from him. "Thanks, Dad." My tiny smile pushes against my bruises and stitches. I hold the bear tightly to my chest. "I'm not hungry yet anyway."

"A Popsicle would have been more helpful," Mom says. "I should have asked Dottie myself when she brought the roses."

Dad looks to her. "Roses?"

"I'm guessing my office or yours." Mom straightens her shirt. "Dottie is keeping them in the staff room until Sarah gets a regular room."

"That's nice, but we don't know who sent them?" Dad asks.

"There wasn't a card," I say, "but your gift is best, Daddy." I know exactly what it means: he loves me.

He grins. Hugely.

Mom fusses with the blinds.

CHAPTER 23

Haddings

3:15 am

I toss one way and then the other. Kick the empty pizza box off the bed and groan along with my indigestion. Yzma swats my leg and leaps off the mattress.

After Cydni's description, horrific images keep crossing my mind, but it's brain damage or limited movement that has got to be Sarah's real concern. In the dark, fears crawl through my brain like ants building a nest.

I cram another pillow over my face, but the images mix with my garlic breath. I jump up, run to the bathroom, but nothing comes up. I'm left with the nausea.

Splashing my face with cold water brings a little clarity. I look in the mirror. "Before, I was worried whether she would live. Now I can worry about her appearance and normalcy." I dry off and admit into the terry cloth, "Or maybe I'm really worried about me?"

I shove the towel hard against my mouth and yell, yell out the anguish, fear, and the whys. I yell until there's no more sound to carve out of my lungs.

CHAPTER 24

Sarah

3:35 am

The clock says 3:35 am. I act like I'm sleeping so Mom will stop fussing over me. Instead, I end up listening in on her and Dad's argument. Who knows which is worse?

"Janet," Dad whispers, "why don't you go home and get some rest with Luke? I'll stay through until morning. You've been here since she was brought in. Take a break."

I peek and see Mom frowning. "I'm not leaving my daughter, Mark, and you shouldn't either," she says.

"Come on, Janet." I can tell Dad's struggling to not sound irritated. "I was only thinking you might need some rest in our own bed."

The tendons in Mom's neck stand out.

"Okay. Forget it!" Dad says. "We'll both stay."

Mom perches on the stool next to my bed like a gargoyle. As she turns toward me, I shut my eyes.

Dad sighs. "I don't know why you insist on putting the worst construction on whatever I say. Why can't you give me the benefit of the doubt at least once?" Someone's stomach grumbles. "Maybe something to eat would reduce the tension," Dad suggests.

"Oh, like a Popsicle?" Mom huffs.

"Well, I'm going to grab some food from the kiosk," says Dad. "Anything I can get you?"

"Coffee," she mutters.

"All right."

I slip to sleep hoping coffee will chill my mother out. For everyone's sake.

3:52 am

Dad's not here, and Mom's sleeping when I wake again. Sitting on the stool, her head rests on my bed. Rain pecks the window behind her.

I lick my dry teeth and try to lift my head. Ow! My neck is cemented stiff.

Without looking, my fingertips discover major bruises down my legs, especially the right one. Didn't they say it took the major hit?

Mom doesn't move as I worm my left hand out from under the sheets and touch my face. The left side feels mostly fine. The right is definitely rashed and covered with goo. I flinch from the tenderness and swelling.

Mom moans.

I wipe the grease on the sheet. The heart machine beeps faster. I walk my weak fingers to my hairline. But my hair's missing. There's the funny haircut. They shaved the front half of my head!

Twisted, stiff knots poke out of my numb scalp. Stitches? My pain below the cut peaks. My fingertips whisper along the dead line from above my left brow down to my right ear. Beyond the fat stitching is baldness. Like all the way to where a headband would go. There's snarled hair behind that, and then it's tangled to the ends. If I tried to brush it, my head would pop open.

Sickened, I slide my trembling hand back under the sheet and silently cry for myself, for me. Beautiful? Isn't that what Mom said at some point? Her compliments have never been emptier. I'm hideous.

No matter what Haddings might be thinking, there's no way he'd be attracted to this. I didn't just have a crush, Cydni; I really cared about him, and it doesn't matter a speck now. Giant, warm tears run off my face.

4:10 am

I'm only sniffling by the time the nurse comes in and wakes Mom. "You can wait here, Janet. We are going to take Sarah down for another CAT scan," explains Marlisa, the new nurse on shift.

"I really don't like her out of my sight," Mom blurts and stands. "Isn't this too much radiation?"

"It's necessary; to be sure the healing is continuing."

Stop already, Mom, I want to say.

"But she's due for pain medication," she argues.

"Yes, we'll take care of that." Marlisa flips switches and unhooks different machines. All the dangling wires look like a depressed octopus. Kind of a reflection of my mother standing there with nothing to do.

Another attendant comes into the room, and I'm being wheeled away. I have to admit a tiny bit of my heart hiccups at being away from my mom. A teensy tiny part.

"Be careful of that corner." She points. "Are you going to miss the corner?" She helps push the bed despite their silence.

"Mom, they know what they're doing. Stop worrying," I say, even though it doesn't help either of us. The bed wheels squeak on the turn, and then I'm gone. Out of Mom's sight. At least I'm not on the heart monitor. It would totally give me away right now.

4:25 am

The CAT scan goes exactly like I remember from before, and I chant, don't pee; don't pee, even though I still have the dumb catheter in. When we are done, another attendant pushes me back through empty halls.

Light, light, tile. Tile, tile, light.

My brain is almost back to shape. How bizarre to see a picture of your brain. Is it going to be okay? One second, I can remember a whole poem, the next, I remember stuff that never happened, and in the next, I can't seem to keep my thoughts on one — light, light, tile. Tile, tile, light. Letter, tile, light. Letter? Poem? And what's the name of my school?

Tile, tile, light.

Back on my floor, I get parked in the hall when Marlisa has to go to the station for a call. I suddenly hear an awful cry, deep from the belly, coming out of my room. Mom? Really? My mom is losing it? And it doesn't sound like anyone is in there with her.

As staff rushes down to the other end of ICU, I lie there and listen in on my mom's grief. Her naked soul shivers my skin, and tears tip from my eyes again.

Finally, she quiets.

When the nurse returns and wheels me into the dark room, Mom's asleep, her feet tucked up and her face pressed against the back of the chair. Her hair is swept across her cheek.

Marlisa smiles at me and hooks me quietly to the machines. The rain covers up most of the clicks and beeps. "I'll bring you that Popsicle now, okay?"

"Sure."

Dad strides into the room with a drink tray and bags of snacks. He opens his mouth but closes it quickly when he sees Mom sleeping. He sets down everything by the sink, then pulls a blanket from the little closet.

"Don't you eat anything your father has brought back," the nurse whispers.

"'kay," I answer. It's not like I really want anything anyway.

She slips out of the room while Dad drapes the blanket over Mom's curled body.

She stirs but doesn't wake. The stool creaks as Dad slowly rolls it to my side. "Your mother means well," my dad says to me in a soft voice.

I nod.

"We need to be patient with her, Sarah." He turns to Mom, reaches out to cover her hand with his, but he withdraws at the last second. Instead, he prays under his breath. "God, there's so much pain clattered inside her. Give her peace in you and patience with everyone else."

Dad looks at me and smiles. He's so hopeful. How, how can he be?

CHAPTER 25

Haddings

5:03 am

I wrap up in my Navajo blanket, sit cross-legged on the braided rug in front of the couch with Yzma, and watch the storm pummel the sliding glass door. The thoughts at the edge of my mind slink forward.

How did Sarah react when she woke — if she woke — and found out I was the one who hit her? I pull the blanket tighter. I'm sure Cydni was the one who told. She could hardly wait, I bet.

So what? Who told doesn't matter. If I could go and face the family and Sarah, would that bring peace? The moon cracks the clouds.

What can I do with these huge heroic resolutions to take care of her? There has to be something.

Yzma purrs and licks my hand. Sarah has so much wit and spark. She loves Dante, Milton, Shakespeare. She's a beauty — or was before the accident — maybe still will be.

I stare up at the ceiling. When she stayed after class and told me UW had sent her an early acceptance, I should have encouraged her to keep thinking about Mills. But I suppose I was really hoping we'd have a chance to be friends at the U. The guilty truth is, I put what I wanted ahead of what was best for her. Her crush made it all so easy.

Lightning illuminates the black corners of the room, and I roll the aches from my neck. Next year, she might easily blindside me.

Yzma presses her head into my palm, nudging me to pet her. I scratch under her chin, and resolve flows through me, head to toe. A little later, I'm going back to the hospital to try to make this right, all of it right. Period.

PART 2

Day Two

CHAPTER 26

Haddings

7:10 am

I wake at my desk, cheek pressed against my laptop, with Yzma's tail draped over my neck and a bottle of antacid filling my vision. My cat leaps down when I shove the bottle aside. The image on my screen reboots.

Mark, Janet, Luke, and Sarah McCormick smile at me from her district speech and debate win, right before Thanksgiving. The report details her victory. These are the faces who may, for all time, hate and despise me. Nerves needle my fingers.

Am I any closer to words that will mean anything when I see these people? Ones that will help Sarah and others, which might touch her parents so they don't sue? I have to try to be practical about everything in the midst of all the emotion. My journal page is empty. Nothing.

Maybe there aren't words.

Yzma lingers by the front door and swipes at a long leaf on my fern.

"Hey!"

She looks at me then reaches up and tears off a piece of the frond with her teeth.

Hopeless.

Sarah's mom stares at me from the picture. Even smiling, the woman has an edge. A lot like Yzma.

CHAPTER 27

Sarah

7:50 am

I wake to Mom dumping the empty snack bags from last night. She pulls the blanket over Dad now, since he's sleeping. She sips what has to be a cup of cold coffee.

"Not too bad," she whispers, holding it out to me. "The nurse said you can have a little now since you kept down the Popsicle and Jell-O. Your stomach seems to be fine after the anesthetic."

I shake my head. "It feels like it, but no thanks. I'll wait for a hot cup with breakfast." I smile at Dad lumped in the chair. "He hardly fits in that recliner."

Mom nods and swirls her cup. "What's he holding?" She peeks between his fingers. "Your CAT scan," she says. Surprisingly, a soft smile touches her face. She doesn't even wake him to grouse that he's curling the edge of the image. The sleep and food definitely did her some good. What a relief.

8:34 am

Dad wakes and stretches when Pamela, another nurse, comes into my room. She quickly explains what she'll be doing to me. "All set then?"

"I think I'll wait in the hall for a bit." Rubbing his stubbly chin, Dad scoots out the door.

"'kay," I answer. There's no way I want him to see this part anyway.

Mom holds my hand tightly but looks at the wall to give me privacy. I was the one who reached out to her without thinking.

Pamela lifts the sheets and grips the catheter. Why in the world does she smell like Fritos so early in the morning? Yuck! I hold my breath.

"You'll just feel a pressure," she says, and pulls.

"Ahhhh," I grit my teeth and blink away tears. The thing is out of me. It's out. It's out! I pant and squeeze my thighs together against the remaining aches. Whoever invented that torture? Man!

Pamela covers me with the blanket and another *whoosh* of chewed chips. Mom turns and dabs my brow, but I pull away. "I'm okay." I let go of her hand. "Dad, you can come in," I call.

"I'll just wait out here until the nurse is done with everything." Mom rolls her eyes.

"All right," I answer. At least he trusts me to deal with this. Well, me and Mom.

Pamela washes her hands. "The oxygen is simple." She pulls

the tube away, and I rub my tickled nose with the back of my hand. "Now, the drainage tube. The doctor said the fluids have slowed from surgery, so you don't need it anymore."

"Isn't this all too fast? I mean, she just had surgery yesterday," says Mom, whose grimace hovers above the nurse's shoulder. And that's when my hands go limp and the room shifts. Talk about Fritos, it's like a Cheeto is being tugged out from under my scalp.

"Ow, ow, ow!" I exclaim as the pain creeps higher and higher.

Air whistles in through Mom's teeth. She reaches for my shoulder, but I shrug her off.

"And some gauze will stop the temporary bleeding." Pamela presses where the tube thingy was in my head. "Deep breath through your nose, and exhale slowly through your mouth."

"Yeah, I got it," I say quickly, to stop her from breathing on me anymore.

"This was the right timing to remove the drainage, Mrs. McCormick. No need to question your surgeon."

"Of course," agrees Mom. "You are doing great, Sarah!"

Sure. It's just that my skull wants to crack open and burp out my brains. I focus on how I'd like to pretty much run over both the driver and Pamela right now.

With her torture completed, Pamela whisks out of the room, and Dad comes in. "Wow. Look at you! Without all those tubes, you look more human already."

Really, Dad? My eyes start to fill, but I try to get it under control as Mom gives him the death stare.

"Oh, no. I meant you almost look like yourself again, except for the shaved head and the stitches ... Uh, right. I'll go see about that breakfast you ordered last night, Sarah." He rushes out of the room before he says anything else. It's almost funny. Almost. Well, not really at all.

Suck it up. No need to lose it and make everything worse between them. I shift in the bed, run my hands along the cold rails.

And that's when I notice. You are kidding me. Seriously? How do I need to pee when the catheter came out only a bit ago? "Mom, I need to use the bathroom," I admit when I can't stand it any longer.

She stops folding the extra blanket and comes around the bed quickly. "Let's sit you up slowly."

Ohhh. There's the Cyclops. He rolls. I had forgotten he was in there. Totally blanked on him, but he's definitely not gone. "Ugh," I moan.

Mom moves the IV stand closer. "Okay. Carefully set your feet down."

"Mom. I know, Mom." I duck from her hand even though my soles are tingling in the fuzzy socks on the freezing linoleum. "I've got it. I can stand. See." I force my legs to hold me up as I push off the bed. Teetering, I grind my teeth but smile through the pain of the Cyclops clubbing my skull.

See through the pain, right through it. Breathe. Take a step to the bathroom. Lift my right foot—whoa! All my strength and energy drain in a flush. I'm going to faint or hurl. "The pan, the pan, Mom!"

She can't reach the puke pan, but she does get the trash can under my face as I fall to a seat on the bed. The jarring unleashes another pain wave. With a strong arm across my back, Mom keeps me sitting upright so I can hurl. While I vomit green spew, a fire fries my head and burns the Cyclops to a crisp.

126

Mom's sane voice drifts through my brain fog. "One thing at a time, Sarah. Let's lie you down. I'm buzzing the nurse. Let's get the sheet up over you. Here's the IV pole closer so the tubing isn't pulled. Here's a cool cloth to wipe your lips. Here's another for your cheek. Just the one side, don't worry. It's nice and cool. It's okay, sweetie. We were just trying to do a little too much. Sarah. Sarah, look at me."

I try, but my eyes want to roll backward instead. Roll back and stay up in there.

"I'm hitting the button again for the nurse, Sarah. Look at me, honey. Breathe, Sarah."

Somehow, I do. I take a breath in.

"Good, good. Deep in through your nose. Let it out."

Between my fluttering eyelids, I spot Pamela hurrying toward me. "Looks like too much too soon." She's checking vitals now. My vision clears, but sight and sound are still in a weird slow motion. "She's okay, Janet."

Mom plops onto the stool. "She can't walk to the bathroom."

"That's understandable considering the circumstances, and that's what a bedpan is for."

Finally, the pain slackens, and the nausea settles. Everything runs on normal speed again. On the hospital pain scale of one to ten, the pain drops to a six. "I'm better," I assure Mom.

However, against every excuse I can think of, or way I can resist them, Mom and Pamela get my dead weight perched on the ridiculous pan. How long will I need help from everyone? It's sick.

I glance at Mom and Pamela waiting for me to pee. They are looking away right now. Would I rather it was Cydni helping me? Definitely not. We are talking peeing here. Some things even best friends shouldn't see.

At least Pamela's had a mint now. And Dad doesn't walk back in on us. It takes like ten minutes to get anything to come out into the pan. Whoever thought peeing would be such a big deal, but the two of them are smiling like I'm two years old with my first success.

It's still completely better than a catheter though.

CHAPTER 28

Haddings

Last second, pathetic fear stalled my early departure, but the delay let me take the lawyer's return call, and I didn't miss it because I was driving. I fall across my bed and repeat what he said. "The police department did not recommend criminal charges, and the prosecutor should follow the cops' lead."

I scrunch my Nerf basketball and bean it at the hoop stuck to the wall. It sails through the net and bounces across the floor. "Yes!" The red ball stops by my foot.

Red. No, not red. Red like the roses in the Burns poem.

I cram my fingers through my hair and sit up. Why didn't I think of the poem when I picked out the flowers for Sarah? Why? Noooo. What about the lines:

I will luve thee still, my Dear,
While the sands o'life shall run.

And I will come again, my Luve,
Tho' it were ten thousand mile!

My stomach burns. Maybe the flowers haven't been delivered yet.

I grab my phone, look up the number for the hospital, and call. Reception transfers me. "Yes, I was calling about Sarah McCormick's status?"

"Just a minute, please."

"Sir?" says a woman.

"Yes?"

"Sir, Sarah is getting ready to be moved to a private room, off the ICU ward, in the late morning."

"Oh, great. So, if I ordered flowers yesterday, they'll be deliv—"

"Did they happen to be a dozen red roses?"

"Yes?"

"They accidently were brought up. My colleague stored them in the break room, but she told me to be sure they are moved with Sarah when she is transferred."

"Oh." I sigh. "So, she hasn't seen them yet."

"Just between you and me, the nurse said she took them down to Sarah for a look, thinking they would encourage her. Are you the sender, sir? Can I transfer your call?"

"No. No thanks. I need to go. Thanks for your help." I tap my phone off.

Sarah saw them. She saw the roses. I cover my face. Even though I left off a card, she'll suspect they are from me. I remember that one day outside the teacher's lounge, she told me she memorized the Burns poem. She'll suspect I sent the flowers, that is, if her brain can remember or process, and she may misconstrue everything again.

So what was her reaction? The nurse didn't say, did she? No. I think she would have mentioned if Sarah tore the flowers to pieces. She said they were safe somewhere, for now. And Sarah was well enough for the nurse to show them to her. That's good, right?

I tug my T-shirt away from my neck. Did I subconsciously want to bring the poem to Sarah's mind?

I catch my reflection in my dresser mirror and sit frozen. "Whatever I truly feel, I know I haven't gone the ten thousand miles." My wall clock ticks, ticks, ticks.

With a deep breath, clarity dawns, creeping light over all my fears, which are suddenly silenced. My own truth steps forward. Boldly.

I jump up and start straightening my sheets, then the covers. I'm going now. It may be hard on the family to see me, but if it's helpful to Sarah, isn't that worth it? As long as it's helpful to her. Couldn't I be? Helpful?

Cydni's certainly wrong. Whenever you foul up everything, there's still a right thing to do, my dad always says.

After carefully dressing, picking out nice clothes to win any points possible with the parents, I down a cup of espresso and a bagel. I'm ready.

Before I realize it, I'm in traffic, forcing my heart to slow as I pass pedestrians. I'll do what I can this second. That means drive to the hospital, see her — them. Talk. Or try for a chance to. And Cydni should be in school. Hopefully.

131

CHAPTER 29

Sarah

9:50 am

When my mom's back is turned, I press my fingers against my puffed face. Despite what the doctor said, there were still fluids from the surgery left to drain. Without the tube in, they are slipping down and swelling my head up like a balloon. The pressure stretches my skin taut, like a frog in a microwave. Why didn't it all drain out earlier? Or why didn't they leave the tube in longer? Maybe Mom was right and not the surgeon? I must be freakish beyond belief.

I jerk my hands down as she faces me. "Done with breakfast?"

"Yeah."

She rolls my tray away. It found its way here before Dad even came back. "You didn't eat much, Sarah."

"Did, too. Some eggs, a couple grapes, and I drank the coffee. I'm full."

"I suppose it's normal to have a small appetite after surgery." She covers the leftovers with the plastic lids.

"Yeah, so go ahead, Mom. Go find Dad and at least let him know he can stop looking for my breakfast. And then get some food. It's not like you'd eat my leftovers."

She looks at my cart. "True."

"Mom, go. You know you get crabby when you don't eat."

"I do not!"

I stare at her through my puffy eye slits.

"All right. You sure you'll be okay without me for a few minutes?"

"Go!" I say, and she actually listens. For once.

CHAPTER 30

Haddings

My back prickles at the timing. Worrying his hands, an elderly man steps out of children's ICU, which allows me to get through the double doors before they lock closed. I didn't have to buzz the desk and possibly get denied entry. I inhale, preparing for whoever might be in the room with Sarah right now.

Clipping through the corridor, I slide right past the nurse's station, with only one woman at the copy machine, working on a paper jam. The air is thick with tragedy in this wing. Room after room holds disorder and pain.

I stop at the door with Sarah's name markered on the board. My legs are petrified wood. I don't hear any voices, so I peek. The room is empty, apart from the bed behind the half-pulled curtain. "Sarah." I tip inside. "Sarah?"

CHAPTER 31

Sarah

10:12 am

I recognize his voice the second time he says my name. "Haddings!" I gasp. Before he gets past the curtain, I yank the sheet up over my face. A blaze combusts between the white fabric and my sticky skin. My poky stitches rake the material.

He cares enough to visit? The hurt for what I'll never have with him spikes my chest, while my pride ratchets up panic. He rejected me with his poem, and now I look like a monster. Squirming under the bedding, I blurt, "I'm, I'm not up for visitors."

"Sarah, you can speak — move your arms and legs?!" he gushes. I hear the curtain slide. "You sound exactly like yourself. It's so good to hear your voice!"

"Um. Yeah, I can move. And talk. Great, huh? But I'm sorry. I seriously don't want people to see me right now."

"How you look doesn't matter to me, Sarah."

"No, believe me. This matters."

There's a long pause, and then he goes, "Sarah, I want you to know I'm sorry. So very sorry about the accident. You have to believe me."

"Yeah. Thanks." I wait a second but don't hear him moving toward the door. "And thanks for coming. It means a lot to me. I'll see you another time." This is so stupid.

"No, I can't leave yet. I need you to know I'm really, really sorry."

"I believe you. I mean, who would want me to get hit?"

"I never did."

"Of course not," I huff. "But talking through a sheet is pretty ridiculous. I'll see you later, 'kay?"

"It's like I told you in class, as your teacher, I care about you, Sarah. I really do care."

Only the blood pulsing in my ear moves with random stabs of pain.

"After this ... even more," he says. The words hang as if suspended in the thick solution in one of my IV bags.

But there's not enough "care" to overlook all this. The words turn in my broken head, and I shove down the hope, which has the idiocy to flicker that we could be more. Maybe at the U. My bashed brains are more idiotic than ever.

"Sarah, I'm so sorry I hit you."

What?

"I'm sorry I hit you, Sarah McCormick," he says, suddenly sobbing.

Wait. What is he saying?

"I just need to help now — as the driver, I need to do something for you."

Haddings hit me? Haddings? I blaze under the sheet. No. I shake my head through the pain. No! A blue Mustang. It was a blue Mustang. That's what Cydni was trying to tell me. Haddings drives a blue Mustang, and he's the one who hit me. It's crazy impossible. Teachers don't hit students. They don't.

"I'm sorry," he blubbers.

"You? You were driving?" I ask, my voice squeaking.

"What? Didn't anyone tell you?"

"No. No one said anything. Just that the driver was a man. That's all I knew. That's it."

"Oh," he groans.

I breathe fast, faster, until I'm close to hyperventilating. I try to sink farther into the bed, away from him, but I get nowhere. "Were, were you aiming for me?"

"What?" he cries. "How could you say that?"

"I don't know." Tears flood my face. I hold my breath. *Pgh*, the air bursts out and right in again.

"How do you feel?" he asks.

"I don't know. Confused? Shocked. Angry." Am I angry? "Yes, I'm mad, Haddings! Really mad! How could you do this to me?"

"Sarah, please," he begs. The bed shakes as he bumps against it, jarring pain through the top of my head. He's standing right over me and doesn't have a clue how much he just hurt me again. "Believe I'm sorry. I know it's too much to ask you to forgive me."

"You've got that right." Doesn't he? Yes. Definitely, yes.

"I need you to know … well, I'm not exactly sure what did happen, but I, I didn't see you. There was a text—"

"I don't want to hear your excuses!" The sheet puffs with my hot breath. "This, all of this, is your fault!"

"It is. It is. I know it, and I know I should have come sooner to support you, or I mean, at least let you know I was here, but I didn't. I couldn't think straight. Cydni said ... Anyway, I was trying not to upset your family, and honestly, I was terrified. That's the real truth, but then this morning I knew, clearly knew, I had to come back." He spews on and on. "Sarah, I was here all yesterday. I didn't go home until they brought you down from recovery. I waited for you into the night. I was—am sick over what I've done." There's a cough and a sob.

I close my eyes. I'm going to start screaming. Any second.

"But today, I had to come back. I didn't know they hadn't told you, but I knew I had to apologize to you face to face."

"No way," I sputter.

"I have to see you, Sarah."

Like what he needs matters? Is he serious? And he wants to talk, face to face? I pant, and my head goes lighter still. Do I let him see, to show for real what he's done, to make him suffer? Will he? Do I look bad enough to twist his guts?

My pride shouts, "Don't! You'll blow the sliver of a chance you have left for someday." But is there a sliver? He said he cares for me. But that was the old me. And who would want to even be friends with a guy who runs you down? I clench my fists tighter. Come on, Sarah. There's ... nothing ... left. Go ahead. Why not see how much he so-call cares.

"Sarah?"

My arms spasm. "Face to face? Take a good long look then." I flip the sheet down. "This is what you did, Haddings."

138

CHAPTER 32

Haddings

10:17 am

My stomach swallows itself. There's an enormous gash from above one eye down to her opposite ear. There are horrific black and red stitches lumped with coagulated blood along the messy lesion. Her wide, bald crown gleams with some kind of ointment. There's a green-black bruising over her immensely swollen, distorted head. I can hardly find her eyes in the beaten flesh.

I start vomiting words. "No, no."

She stares at me through puffed eyelids, nearly compressed closed.

"There's no way I did this, Sarah. No! No way."

Wonder, anger, and rage cross her teeny eyes. "Oh, right. So what's left? You think I stepped in front of your car on purpose?"

I'm shocked motionless.

"Like your poem freaked me out so bad that I tried to kill myself?"

CHAPTER 33

Sarah

10:18 am

Everything focuses to a pinpoint. The disbelieving rage burns from my mouth. "You think, you think I'm that pathetic?"

He shakes his head. "No," he whispers. "I never would think that. No!"

I pound my fists against the bed. The tape on my IV is tugged from my skin. I grimace and mash it back down. "You think my life doesn't have meaning anymore just because you aren't willing to risk anything for me? Even after I turned eighteen? Because I know you were attracted to me. I know it, no matter how much you deny it and talk about stupid boundaries. You were."

Haddings jerks back. "No, that's not true, Sarah. I've told you the truth all along. Okay, I shouldn't have given you extra

141

attention—you're just such an amazing student—and I should have encouraged you to go to Mills and not the U next year with me—"

"Don't flatter yourself. Maybe I had other reasons for considering UW besides you." I snort. "And what does any of it matter, anyway, since you hit me. Face it. You."

He crumples into the chair and weeps.

For the first time ever, he disgusts me, for so many reasons.

CHAPTER 34

Haddings

I heave in air and stew in the anguish. It was me. "I'm a fool, on so many counts, Sarah."

Suddenly, my chest lightens with a small glow deep inside as I hear what she said. Not that I ever believed it, but my mom put the ridiculous doubt deep in the back of my mind. Sarah didn't throw herself in front of my car because of what I did, or said, or didn't do. It … was an accident.

CHAPTER 35

Sarah

10:20 am

My ball of anger burns like an exploding star. He hit me because he wasn't looking. My swollen head is going to flame, all the medicines and antiseptics will torch before I collapse into a black hole.

I snuffle my tears into the sheet because I can't reach the stupid tissues on the window sill. Finally, my anger sizzles down, down, down, leaving behind a heavy blanket of weakness.

Why isn't he leaving after I've yelled at him? I look over. He's all curled up, weak, nothing like the guy I thought was so hot that first day in class.

I sniff. Just a guy. Maybe sorry for what he did, or said, or didn't do.

The tiniest sprout of sympathy pokes the hot black casing around my heart. And then burns up.

CHAPTER 36

Haddings

Get it together! I pull a tissue from the nearby box. I swipe it over my face as awkwardness oozes through the cramped room.

"I'm so, so sorry, Sarah."

She glances at me then looks away.

"And I'm sorry I wasn't here when you woke. I should have been here."

She barely shrugs. "The people who still care for me were here."

A knife gouges and flicks a bit of my heart to the floor. "Yes, I saw them earlier ... yesterday."

She wipes her nose on her gown.

I hand her a tissue, and she takes it. My fingers softly wisp against hers, and she flinches. I rub my neck. "My parents and

I, we'll pay for everything. We'll find a way, even if it takes time, the rest of my life."

She glances down at the bed and picks lint off the blanket. "Yeah, well, that's great, but it doesn't help my face, or the rest of my messed-up body." She lifts her head. "It doesn't tell me that my brain is okay, and that I'll still be able to graduate and go to college. It doesn't pay a cent for any of that." She snorts.

"Well, we'll see. I mean, first things first. I can meet with your family, Sarah. I'll apologize and offer everything I have and do anything I can."

"Um, no way. They don't want to see you — believe me." She scoots down. "Look, I'm super tired. I'll tell my folks you were here if that's what you want, but you need to leave before they get back."

I hesitate.

"I'm serious. Stay away so everyone can cool down. It could be bad." Her voice quiets. "Now would you go? It's too much." With the blanket pulled to her chin, she tears up again.

"Okay, if that's what you want." I step to the door. "I'm so sorry."

She turns her face away. "Go."

I do.

CHAPTER 37

Sarah

10:28 am

In the quiet, I slowly start to breathe normally again. "Haddings hit me," I whisper, blow my nose, and close my eyes. Hey, Cydni. Haddings and I might have been friends next year at the U, and it might have finally gone somewhere. You know what? I always believed it would happen eventually, no matter what you said. Before. Before I was hit. I tuck my chin and silently cry it out.

A short bit later, my mom bursts into my room. She stops a second at the sink to wash her hands. "I didn't find your father, but I found a Starbucks and a scone. Are you happy?" She glances over. Obviously, she can see I've been upset, but she doesn't mention it. I've been weepy since I woke from surgery.

My breath comes out shaky. "Absolutely."

Right then, my dad rolls a tray into the room, victorious

in his quest. "I found your breakfast!" He whips off the metal plate covers. "Voilà! Breakfast for a princess!"

"A frog princess, maybe," I counter.

Even Mom smiles while drying her hands.

"Um, Dad. I don't know whose that is, but I already had mine. See?" I point to my tray.

Before we can get the food figured out, and who's missed out on a meal with Dad's find, or I decide whether or not to tell my folks about Haddings, the staff descends and begins to switch me out of ICU.

As they roll me down the hall, I keep my eyes closed to the other kids crying in their rooms. "Here are your roses," says Marlisa, but I don't look. I can't. They mean absolutely nothing. Maybe that was some little inkling of Haddings' heart slipping out, even subconsciously, but it doesn't matter now in the least.

"I'll carry those," Dad offers.

"Take care now," she says.

"Thanks," I reply, barely peeking at her. The attendants move me two floors below, into a private room overlooking Seattle.

A new nurse named Qwan welcomes us and helps Dad scoot me off the one bed into the clean new one. Mom scurries to cover the mirror with all the balloons and flowers that were delivered.

When I'm settled in the space and Qwan leaves, I tell my folks about Haddings' visit. "So, yeah. I know who hit me now, and that's pretty much what happened when he was here." I leave out what I hoped was between the two of us before, and what could have happened one day but won't. "I really wish you had told me right away. I can't believe Cyndi didn't at least."

"No. We told her not to. It was right not to," says Mom,

148

shoving her hair behind her ear. "Look how much worse knowing made everything."

"Forget it. I don't want to talk about it," I say.

She paces. "The nerve of him coming here. Sneaking in when you were alone."

"He wasn't sneaking, Mom. You guys just weren't here."

Dad squeezes a balloon so tightly it pops, and we all jump.

"I shouldn't have left you alone." My mother crosses her arms.

"No, Mom. I'm—it's fine." I was right. Haddings better not come around for a long, long time.

Dad gazes across the gray cityscape to the Sound. "So he's twenty-one?"

"Yeah. He, like, graduated early through homeschooling, finished college, and is in his first year of grad school now." Things I found out from him over our lunch at the U.

"A kid."

"It doesn't matter." Mom wipes at a smudge on the sink. She shoves the paper towel into the garbage. "He's going to pay."

"Of course he'll have to pony up." Dad slips his hands into his pockets. "Imagine his parents. They have it easier than we do, but this has to be pretty awful for them as well." He turns and looks at me. Mom refuses to reply.

11:45 am

When my mother's friends call and ask if they can visit, I nod yes. Since Haddings saw me, who cares who else does?

The ladies arrive with more flowers, more balloons, and some magazines. The gorgeous models seem to sneer at me, while my mom's friends stand there shocked.

149

"Thanks," I mumble, "for the gifts and ... stopping by."

Nancy manages to smile first. "Oh, our pleasure." She and Pat hug Mom and give sympathetic looks to Dad.

"Has she asked to see herself?" Nancy whispers to Mom, who shakes her head.

"No, I don't want to see what I look like. I just don't," I say quickly.

"And that's fine." Mom pats my arm. "There's no rush."

Pat fills the silence. "There's so much to be thankful for. It could have been much worse."

I tuck my chin, probably making the stitches easier to see, and the room goes silent again.

Gossip does bubble up when they think I've fallen asleep. Nancy says, "Did you hear what happened over at Auburn High?"

Pat cuts in. "Are you talking about the PE teacher caught with the student?"

"Yes!"

"What?" Mom asks.

"Can you say pedophilia?" Nancy adds with what must be a pop of her lips.

"Are you serious?" Mom straightens my sheet, but I don't open my eyes, so they'll keep talking.

Pat fills in that a teacher had sex with a freshman in his car. "All caught on the security camera!" she whispers.

"No," Mom says.

Dad's silent through all this. What is he thinking?

"That girl's poor parents," Nancy adds, but clarifies, "not that it compares to your trial."

I struggle to lie completely still. The ladies chitter on about the teacher being charged. Even short of sex, this is the sort of ridicule, or actual risk, Haddings would have been under with me — if anyone found out. Which is ridiculous, since we are both adults, but this is what Cydni was hinting at, what I never wanted to hear. The risk was real.

Everything might have tipped that one day if Cydni hadn't walked in on us. It was totally against Haddings' "I can't be alone with a student" rule, but he didn't leave when I came to class early, did he? He looked incredibly hot sitting on his desk, reading a verse novel. I could see the tension in his hands though as he set the book aside and picked up a yardstick and fiddled with it. He was as determined not to respond as I was determined to get him to. It was like a showdown, proving I couldn't get to him or something.

"You're early," he said, "and no one else is here yet."

I shrugged and walked through the empty room, stopping before him. "It will only be a minute before they show up."

The yardstick bounced in his hands, tapped the carpet, tapped around my Chucks, and skimmed the inside of my bare ankles.

I handed him my journal. "So, I checked out 'Song of Solomon.'"

"From the Bible?"

"Yep. Most beautiful love poem ever," I said and quoted, "Let him kiss me with the kisses of his mouth; For thy love is better than wine." I nudged the ruler aside with my knee and inched forward.

He leaned back on one hand. "Thy teeth are like ewes that are newly shorn."

We busted up laughing. "I go to church, you know," I said when our giggling petered off.

151

"Really?" he answered.

"Uh huh."

"And you learn about right and wrong?"

"Yeah." I bit my lower lip. "Mostly." I looked at him through my lashes and pressed forward against the edge of the desk. His knees burned my hips.

Haddings sat still as if he had no other choice, a sailor to a siren. The small gap between us aflame.

And then Cydni banged open the dumb door. Haddings quickly nudged me away and slipped past me.

I stood still while the dizziness and sizzle were chased away by the bell. Cydni's glares helped me make my way to my seat as the other kids streamed in. Desire rolled after my heels, despite my best friend's disapproval.

But then a few weeks later, when Haddings read his ridiculous poem, I couldn't look at him. After class, Cydni caught me by the arm and steered me to lunch.

I got right into it. "What do you think he meant when—"

"It's obvious, Sarah. Never. Be happy alone. Couldn't be clearer." She bumped me forward with her tray in the cafeteria line.

But I couldn't let it go. The night before his next session with us, just two nights ago, I copied out a poem for him.

That morning, he hit me with his car. Cydni never warned me that could happen.

My thoughts break when mom's friends' discussion turns to Haddings. "Who is he anyway? A grad student? What was the PTA thinking funding this poet-in-residence? This should be a school board decision, don't you think?"

"And what was he doing to hit a child in the crosswalk?"

"The imbecile!"

"Who doesn't see a kid crossing the road?"

I snap open my eyes and glare at Mom's friend for being that harsh to Haddings — what business is it of hers anyway — and for calling me a kid.

Dad catches me wiping angry tears off my chin.

Nancy raises her nose. "He definitely shouldn't be in a position of authority over our children!"

Dad closes his book and interjects for the first time since the ladies arrived. "That was, uh, my first thought, too." He rushes on. "Especially when I saw Sarah, I was ready to destroy the kid. Well, teacher. Kid really, though, right? Twenty-one."

I nod, even though he uses the word "kid," too.

"Anyway," Dad says, "after considering everything, I realized it could have happened to any of us."

Each lady stops mid-breath.

"What I mean is that any one of us could have been the driver. I've taken a call on my cell. I've pulled something from the glove box, or I've zoned out driving because of some distraction. You know, Janet, how it is when I have a Mariners game on."

Mom and her friends glare at Dad. He rubs his chin. "I'm only saying it could have been one of us driving. Maybe we shouldn't be so quick to judge. Sarah could have been driving. Heaven forbid, but even she could be 'the driver' one day."

"Mark!" Mom stands and takes my hand. I pull out of her grip. "Don't defend that man when he did this to Sarah!"

The women glower.

"No, of course not. I just wanted to share what I've been thinking. Thoughts about trying to forgive and be charitable. Certainly, all of us should be focused when we are driving.

There's no excuse for this accident, so believe me, I'm not defending him."

There's a group sigh, and the chitchat resumes, but I still stare at Dad. Even when Mom tells her friends she'll be sleeping in my room with me, when I'm released—as if—I don't get distracted or return Dad's little smile.

He bends down and whispers to me. "It's better all around to concentrate on getting better."

I force a nod through my confusion. One second I'm ticked at the women for slamming Haddings, and then the next I'm mad at Dad for cutting him slack. Really? He doesn't think I'd see someone in a crosswalk? Under a streetlight?

How much would Dad sympathize with Haddings if I announced the guy used to be attracted to me? Dad would fume like Mount St. Helens in the eighties. There'd be no more lectures about who could have been driving and stuff like that.

I try to pull my anger away from Dad and throw it back on Haddings, but I'm too tired. Tired of all of it, especially the visitors. It's a relief when Pat and Nancy say good-bye.

I eat a bit for lunch then, finally, I zonk out for real. For at least an hour, I escape everything: the pain, the awkwardness, the stares, the need for help. I'm gone.

1:45 pm

Unfortunately, I wake feeling stiffer than ever. It's amazing I can yawn since my face feels tighter than before. I blink to focus.

Dad's standing right next to me. There's a big black garbage bag on the chair at his side, and my mom's looking at it like it's a bomb. "Feel better?" he asks.

I shrug. "What's that?"

He pats the sack. "It's all your stuff from the accident, Sarah. The police brought it in while you were napping."

Mom disappears into the bathroom.

The poem for Haddings! Maybe it's still in my pocket. I reach for the bag.

"Let me help you," says Dad. He loosens the tie and lifts it onto my bed. "Now, what do you need?"

"Nothing! Can I just look inside?" I don't wait for an answer and root around for my pants. Got 'em! My fingers slide under the snap and curl around the note deep in the pocket. Unbelievably, it's still there. I tug it free and palm it as Dad reaches in.

"Pink sweatshirt," he says quietly, pulling it out. "You were wearing a pink sweatshirt. I won't ever not stop and notice again."

"It's okay, Dad."

"No, it's not," he says, setting the muddy hoodie aside. He tugs my shredded jeans out next.

I turn from it all and clasp my note under the sheet.

"What's that you have there?" he asks.

I freeze.

"What?"

He points to my fist below the sheet. "What's that?"

"Oh, this?" I pull my hand out. "Just, you know, a note for someone."

He waits.

"It's kind of private, and I was hoping I hadn't lost it."

He nods. "I can see that. You must have been worried."

"Oh, you know." I squirm my hand below the sheet again. "I'm glad to get it back."

155

"Nothing I should be concerned about?"

I slowly shake my head.

"Nothing I should read?"

"No," I whisper.

"Can I deliver it for you?"

"No. Thanks."

His eyes lock onto mine, and he lets me off the hook. He pulls out my cell. It's totally dead.

I shiver. "Everything's so gross." I push the pile away. "I remember throwing up."

"For good reason."

"You know what, Dad? I really don't want to look at everything right now. Would you take the bag away?"

"Sure thing." He quickly reloads it and cinches the sack closed.

Mom comes out of the bathroom while Dad is sliding the bag under my bed. He says, "I'll take this home next trip."

Mom speaks like she's pulling a big, beaded necklace out of her mouth. "That's — a — really — thoughtful — idea — Mark." She doesn't look at him, but he beams.

I slide the note into my sock. With a little nod to the bathroom, Mom understands. "No way do I want to use that bedpan anymore," I say.

"You might not need to." She helps me sit and then stand. "So far, so good." As I take one step and then the next, she rolls my IV pole along beside me. "Look how strong she is, Mark. Look at her!" Mom is so excited, she may wet herself. "A little food makes all the difference, don't you think?"

"Uh huh." Dad comes along the other side of me. With them holding me steady, I make it all the way to the door with only a tiny threat of fainting.

"There's no mirror in the bathroom," Mom points out.

"'kay, great," I say.

Dad goes back to the chair.

"I'm fine," I say after Mom helps get me all the way into the space.

"You are so strong today!" she says and claps. I stare at her. "Oh, sorry." She closes me in. "Call me when you're done."

"I will." I struggle and pull the note from my sock. It's exactly what I wanted to say:

To Mr. Haddings:

[i carry your heart with me (i carry it in]
by e. e. cummings

i carry your heart with me(i carry it in
my heart)i am never without it(anywhere
i go you go,my dear;and whatever is done
by only me is your doing, my darling)
                    i fear
no fate(for you are my fate, my sweet)i want
no world(for beautiful you are my world,my true)
and it's you are whatever a moon has always meant
and whatever a sun will always sing is you

here is the deepest secret nobody knows
(here is the root of the root and the bud of the bud
and the sky of the sky of a tree called life; which grows
higher than soul can hope or mind can hide)
and this is the wonder that's keeping the stars apart

i carry your heart(i carry it in my heart)

I tear the note to little bits and flush them down the toilet. Through the door, Mom asks, "Are you okay, Sarah?"

I don't answer.

"I think she's crying, Mark."

"She's going to cry as she recovers. Let her be."

"Is it the pain, Sarah?" she asks. "Your meds should kick in any second."

I cram toilet paper against my mouth to muffle my sobs.

"Was it seeing your clothes from the accident? Maybe that's making the trauma fresh again?"

I still don't reply, but eventually do open the door. Mom's standing there holding the mauve puke pan for some reason. She tucks it under her arm, and she and Dad walk me to the bed.

I try to stand taller but can't. I'm hunched by the pain and death of a dumb dream. The clichéd hope of love of how many stupid girls? Run down in a moment. Hit.

I catch a blurry glimpse of my face flicking on the doorknob. I close my eyes to the flash in the metal strip that edges the doorway. Am I as gross-looking as those slim reflections hint? I curl up in bed.

What do I really look like half bald? Do I want to know?

2:20 pm

A while later, I'm in another nightmare. "Come on, sweetie. Name three things that start with 'T.'" Mom's begging now.

"Sarah, are you focused?" the therapist asks.

"Uh. Yeah."

"Totally, truly, terribly, ton, tan, tin, top, truth, tell, talk, talk, talk, Sarah!" Mom blasts out.

158

The therapist stares at her. "Please, Mrs. McCormick. This is for Sarah to recall. You're confusing her and taking the words yourself."

"I'm sorry." Mom covers her mouth, and Dad tries to massage her shoulders, but she shrugs him off.

I try my hardest. "I guess I can only think of—"

"Show us your brain isn't damaged, sweetie," says Mom. "You have the Mills scholarship waiting for you." She smiles at the frowning therapist.

Really? She's going to push Mills in the middle of this stupid test? "Two?" I come up with. "I'm sorry. My head hurts is all. I can't concentrate right now."

"That's okay, Sarah." The therapist scribbles notes.

"You're just—tired," Mom stresses.

I close my eyes.

"No worries," says Dad. "Just tired."

I hear the therapist get her stuff together and leave. So what? I failed the dumb test. I remembered a whole stinking poem earlier. The therapist didn't ask me to recite poetry. No, it's "T" words. It's not like I really couldn't think of, um, words. Or, the name of my ... school. Man, what is it?

Anyway, my mom just said the "T" stuff. And my head hurts, and I'm tired, and I didn't feel like trying. I can do it.

Maybe if Cydni was here I could have concentrated. Yeah. "T" words. I open my eyes and look around the room. Nothing sparks my mind, but surely I could think of a thousand or so if I really wanted. Panic bubbles in my blood.

Dad squeezes my foot, and Mom takes my hand. I pull away from her. She's, like, constantly hanging on to me. I want to rip out all these wires and scream every "T" word in the dictionary. If I could only think of them.

Dad picks up his book and finds his place. Mom tucks the blanket around me, then plumps my pillow, offers me water. I don't take it.

Next, she gently begins to comb out the tippy ends of my hair. "Now that looks pretty, Sarah."

I roll my head away from her. "Mom, stop."

She sits on the edge of the bed. "Sarah, please. I think I can work on some of these tangles. If we don't get them out, they'll only get worse. Look." She holds up the hank she was working on. "See how beautiful your hair still is?"

I take the comb from her. "Yeah, right," I scoff. "I don't want my hair combed, Mom. Would you please just give me some space?"

She actually chuckles.

"Mom!" I try to push myself upward, but can't with my weak arms.

"Let me." She reaches to help pull me up.

"Stop!" I say.

"Sarah, it takes humility to admit that you need help."

I huff. "Whatever, Mom. I can tell you I don't have enough humility to stand you sleeping in my room when I go home. I can't believe you said that to your friends!"

Dad turns a page and looks over at the two of us.

Mom's voice wobbles. "It would just be for a while. To be sure you were okay through the night. I need to listen that you are breathing regularly. I can get you anything you might need."

I cross my arms. "No. I don't need you to sleep in my room.

I'm serious, Mom, and, and I'll choose my own college if I get to go. I'm sick of you bringing up Mills."

"But there's no book art degree at—" Her eyes brim. I refuse to answer, and soon she admits the truth of it all. "Before the surgery, you needed me, Sarah."

"I was drugged."

Dad moves between Mom and me. "Some respect, baby girl?"

I look from him to her and lower my voice. "Mom, stop. Please. I'm okay, and while you are at it, you might as well face the truth. Look at me. There's no way I'm beautiful." Now my eyes well up.

"You'll always be—"

"Mom!"

She rips a tissue from the box and swipes her tears. She's going to talk no matter what I say. "The fact is you will always be my beauty, Sarah. No matter what." She twists the Kleenex and starts tearing bits off and balling them up. "And it's just that … I have to say it felt good to feel needed again, beyond a meal, or a ride, or clean socks. I had you for a day, Sarah. You needed me like you haven't for years." She chucks the torn tissue wad and pieces into the trash and walks over to the window, chewing her lip, arms crossed over her chest.

Dad follows and presses ChapStick into her hand.

What can I even say to that? Yay that I needed you? I'm so glad you had a purpose again? My cracked-open head was totally worth it so you could feel good about yourself. Is she serious?

The surgeon comes in and interrupts our silence with his cheery hello. Mom sits down on the stool right by my bed. I ignore her and concentrate on the doctor, washing his hands, then studying my clipboard.

"Your last CAT scan looks very good, Sarah." He hangs up my chart then checks my head. Poking, dabbing, prodding. "So, there shouldn't be that much pain now," he says, stepping over to the sink and washing again.

"What?" Dad starts. "With that enormous incision across my daughter's head. How can it not—"

Without looking up, the doctor goes on. "There are no nerves in the skull or brain. Sarah will only be feeling the skin heal."

"That's good," Mom says.

"How can you be serious? Look at my daughter! How can she not have much pain?"

"Mark, please," Mom says.

The doctor goes on despite Dad. "Tylenol should be sufficient once her IV is removed."

"And would Tylenol be sufficient for your daughter after brain surgery?"

What is up with Dad, going all Chuck Norris? The minute it's about me, taking care of me, he gets all heated up. Will he always doubt the surgeon, man to man?

The doctor turns away and discusses something with the nurse standing in the doorway.

"Uh, Dad," I say.

"Yeah?"

"You're twisting the head off my bear."

He drops it on the bed, and I giggle for the first time since the accident.

"Everything looks good, Sarah." The surgeon spins around again and smiles at me in particular. "We may be getting you home as soon as tomorrow, with a few follow-up, in-home nurse visits."

"Oh, that's great!" I say, while Mom and Dad stand there with their mouths hanging open.

Cydni's mother pops in as the surgeon is leaving. She snaps my parents back to the moment, and they leave the zombie look behind.

"Oh, sweetheart," Chantelle says at the sight of me.

"Swollen from the fluids," I answer.

She shakes her head as Mom relays what the staff has said today. "Lastly," she announces with a sweep of her arm, "they are considering sending her home tomorrow."

"Tomorrow?" Chantelle asks, not hiding the shock in her voice.

Mom nods. "Of course, that's wonderful, as long as it's safe."

"As long as it's safe," Dad echoes.

"Well, it would be awesome to be in my own bed and not have the nurses constantly checking me. Super great to be in my room. Alone," I add, staring at Mom.

She ignores me. "Earlier, I caught the neurologist again, and he clarified Sarah's mind maybe isn't clear because of the anesthetic, or exhaustion, or the surgery itself. She might recall, say, something that wasn't reality. Isn't that what I told you he said, Mark, when we were switching rooms?"

"Yes, that's right."

"Mom, I'm right here. You're talking like I'm not here, and you might have told me that, you know."

"You have enough to focus on, Sarah," she patronizes me.

Mom raises her eyebrows at Chantelle, who asks behind her Kleenex, "The flute?"

My mother nods.

Dad jumps in. "Sarah's eager to do things to help her brain reconnect."

163

"Oh yeah, Dad. Woohoo," I deadpan.

Mom adds, "We'll need to play cards, games, and do crossword puzzles to exercise her mind and check out her capabilities."

"That sounds like fun, Sarah," Chantelle says eagerly.

"Maybe when I'm feeling better. I love solitaire. Right, Mom?"

CHAPTER 38

Haddings

3:10 pm

In the late afternoon, I park facing Alki Beach along West Seattle and turn off my car. The sun is dropping already. The pale waves lap the shore without much energy, although the salty tang in the air is already slipping into my car. It's quickly replacing the heater's lingering warmth.

The lawyer explains, "The parents are undecided regarding a civil suit. One only wants expenses covered; the other insists on leaving the door open as future unknown costs accrue. They have a year to file."

"Okay. Thank you."

"You're welcome. Let me know if you have any more questions."

"I will." Tapping off my phone, I wonder how much that

little conversation cost me. I can't think about a civil suit right now.

I shiver and unbuckle my seat belt, getting the pressure off my indigestion. A ferry slices through the Sound as the sun shimmers at the top of the Olympic Mountain range. In the midst of the stillness, it feels like I could shatter from the tension, like the shards of sea glass scattered among the pebbles. I have a year of this waiting and wondering?

Stifle the pity. Sarah's got it much, much worse. All because of me.

It's incredible that, despite all my effort, she still thinks I was attracted to her. Could she feel it? Despite everything I was telling her and myself, regardless of what I did, safeguarded, and believed, she intuited the opposite.

I lay my head on the steering wheel and watch the gulls circle outside, crying aimlessly. Back in January, Sarah came into class glowing. Before I could ask why, Clayton announced, "Yo, it's Sarah's eighteenth b-day today." The class hooted, and George added, "Legal adult," when he strolled past and bumped knuckles with her.

She glided into her seat and beamed at me. Legal, but still off limits, I countered silently.

A gull chases another across the sand. That was probably the day the crack opened in my heart, and I've been plastering it subconsciously since ... which was still the right thing to do.

The ferry lets out a low tone, and it sounds as lonely as me.

CHAPTER 39

Sarah

4:40 pm

Chantelle couldn't stay long, but she said Cydni should be here soon. She gave me a soft hug before leaving. I've always loved her hugs.

Now, I smugly smile as Mom talks to Grandmother on the hospital phone. "No, it wouldn't be good for you to come right now, Mother."

She yanks the cord to untangle it. I can actually hear my grandmother's answer, she's talking so loudly. "But are you sure, Janet? I can be there very soon to help you."

"No. Everything is complicated right now, Mother. Your flying in wouldn't help."

"Now, Jan-Jan, that can't be true. Don't you worry about your father. He'll manage fine being alone for a few weeks. I'll get a ticket for this weekend. I can take a shuttle from the airport, and I'll be there to cook and clean at the very least. When Sarah comes home, you'll need an extra pair of hands."

"Mother, no—"

"None of that now. You need me, Jan-Jan. A mother always knows. I'll call you with my flight details. Give my love to everyone, especially Sarah. Bye-bye now."

Click.

Mom clatters the phone into the cradle. "Why doesn't that woman ever listen to me?" she mutters.

"Yeah, like that's so weird," I say, snuggling down.

She raises one eyebrow at me, then goes on. "So your dad went home to catch a nap while you were resting, and you missed Pastor Hodgins and Pastor Kelly. They stopped by to check on you."

I yawn. "That's nice. You could have woken me, you know."

"They said not to, which was sweet, but I have to say, the hints about forgiveness were tedious."

I squint thinking about it, but then I can't see out at all between my puffed lids. "Seriously, Mom? They were talking about forgiveness when I'm lying here like this?"

She nods and sits on the edge of the chair. "Of course, they were definitely compassionate and sympathetic the whole time. Still, they were encouraging me to set a good example for you."

"Man, forgiveness seems so far way," I confess.

"Farther than I can imagine." Mom mutes the TV when a short, freckled guy in a brown suit knocks on the door.

"Can I help you?" Mom stands.

"I wanted to speak with you about Sarah's accident," he says. After fake small talk, the man spins how we need to sue the

168

driver, and he can get us a lot of money if we ask him to be our personal injury lawyer.

Mom cuts him off three times. "Thank you," she says, "but my husband has already talked to our family lawyer. Right now we're going to concentrate on Sarah getting better."

This guy doesn't get it or give up. Mom finally sits and waits out the long spiel. She takes his embossed card and then drops it in the garbage as soon as he leaves. "I may have a hard time forgiving Haddings, but I won't run the system to fleece him."

"But will you sue him, Mom?"

My mother turns to me, grips the mustard-yellow water carafe, and fills my cup. The ice rattles in the now-empty container as she clunks it down. "I'll say this once, and then we are going to leave it. We don't know what expenses we could be looking at still. Mr. Haddings' insurance may top out, and we may not be able to afford the costs. We will have college expenses" — she pauses a second, her voice wobbly — "wherever you choose to go."

Will we? I can't even think of "T" words.

Mom continues. "Even if you take the scholarship to Mills—"

"Really? Again?"

She raises her hands. "I'm just saying as an example, even if you take the Mills scholarship, there will be additional costs. Then Luke is right behind you a year later, hopefully at Washington State University. We can't close the door on filing a suit. That's all I'm going to say." She takes the pitcher and walks out.

On the TV, someone instantly wins ten thousand dollars on a game show. That's incredibly unfair.

I sulk. She just had to bring up Mills one more time. Mills, Mills, Mills.

Staring at the white ceiling, I try to figure it all out, separate from my mom and what she's pushing. I don't want to say no, just because she's saying yes. What is it I want, or what's the best choice for me?

The creative writing, book art degree at Mills did look amazing, super specialized. I could learn to craft books for my own poetry. The thought of creating something physically to hold my writing is super appealing. And book crafting is a dying art. Would I miss studying that at the U? Would I ever have the chance to learn it if I didn't go to Mills? Not with the same intensity, for sure. I'd get the creative writing part at UW. Is that enough?

If I ignore Mom and her pushing, I can recall Mills was my first choice before Haddings. There was no question back then. Even my bashed brain remembers that. If I get to go anywhere, where would I choose right this minute?

5:10 pm

The instant Luke and Cydni walk in, the words blow right out of my brother. "Whoa, Sarah! You're like a monster toad. A balloon head." He turns kind of green himself.

Tears plop out of my eyes. This is his greeting the first time I see him since waking from surgery? At least from what I can remember.

Mom's stares laser beams at him. "Oh," he mutters. "I, um, didn't imagine you could look worse than yesterday is all."

"Oh, don't listen to him, Sarah." Cydni slips close to my bed. "He's kidding. It's just the swelling, right, Mrs. McCormick?"

"That's right," Mom agrees.

Luke quickly hides behind a giant card so he doesn't have to look at me. "Hanae gave this to me to give to you. It's from speech and debate, I guess."

"Cool. Bring it here so I can read it." I challenge his gutlessness.

"Here. I want to see, too." Cydni saves him. She retrieves the card and brings it over to me. She reads me every scrawled note and signature while Luke sits down on the chair by the window.

"Hey, you have so many fewer machines today," Cydni notices. "That must mean you are doing better!"

"Yeah." I try to mirror her cheer but fail. Instead, I lick my swollen lips like a disgusting toad. The pain peaks all the sudden, and Cydni dabs my tears with a tissue.

Mom steps to Luke and stiffly pats his back. Suddenly, her touch softens along with her face. She halfway smiles. "It's hard to see Sarah like this, isn't it?" she asks him.

He shrugs.

She goes on. "I know it hurts you. A memory just came to mind, actually."

Luke looks like he wants to bolt. How is Mom going to embarrass Mr. I'm-So-Cool?

"Remember your reaction to your sister when you were little and she fell off her bike?"

"No."

"You were what? Maybe seven?" Mom tucks him close to her side. "You couldn't look at her. You couldn't face her until her lip had nearly healed."

171

"Mom! It's no big deal." He glances at Cydni.

"You've always been my sensitive one," she continues. "We'll give you some time to deal with this. Everyone's different, Luke. We all know how much you love Sarah. Here." She digs through her purse. "Why don't you go buy an ice cream sundae from the cafeteria for Sarah? Her appetite's coming back, and I don't think it will spoil her dinner. You'd like that, right, Sarah?"

"I guess."

"Cydni, would you mind showing Luke the way?" Mom asks, but my friend hesitates. "Just because we were there yesterday."

Luke jumps up. "Yeah, you can show me, Cydni. Come on."

"Is that okay?" She stalls. "I don't have to go, Sarah. It's no problem to stay, if you'd rather I do that."

"No. It's fine. Go. We can talk when you get back. You can fill me in on everything at ... Kentlake." That's the name of my school! I smile at my secret victory. And if she goes, it will give me time to figure out what I'm going to share with her about today. Maybe not everything, with Luke around.

"It's a plan," says Cydni.

Luke grabs Mom's wad of ones, Cydni's hand, and is out the door in a second flat. Wait. Her hand? No, that would be crazy. I lay the card down. "He can hardly look at me, Mom."

She picks at her chipped pink nail polish. She never wears chipped polish. "He's just scared. It scares him to see you so hurt, honey. Same reason your other friends have stayed away, most of mine, and your dad's, too. It's hard to come and see what's happened to someone you love. Some people can't get past their own fears. We're all different. Everyone's doing what they can."

"I guess it's something that Haddings showed up."

Mom doesn't answer, so I go back to my card.

"Oh my gosh!" someone squeals.

I lean forward. Ironically, six girls from Pep Club are crammed in the doorway, the most popular girls that manage to stay far away from me at school.

"Can we come in?" their president, Kara, asks.

Mom looks to me, and I shrug. "Sure, girls," she says, and motions to them then adjusts the neck of my gown. "It's so nice to have Sarah's friends visit. Thank you for coming!"

"Of course," says Kara.

"Sarah?" Anna gapes.

"Yikes! Does that hurt?" Willow asks.

"I can't believe what happened to you!" Anna adds.

"I can't even tell it's you, Sarah!" says Laura.

I stop registering who's saying what until Kara says, "I can't believe Mr. Haddings did this to you."

I raise my voice over theirs. "It was a total accident!" I hold my breath to bottle my tears. It's a good thing Cydni isn't here to hear me defend him.

"Oh, we know. I mean" — Anna runs her hand down her reddish blonde ponytail — "everyone knows Haddings is near perfect. We're all just hoping he gets to come back and teach."

"Well, what matters right now is you," Kara says. "I can't believe how horrible you, or, I mean, this all is." Everyone adds their adjectives.

I turn my head and tug my sheet to my neck. My stupid lips go blubbery. Mom nudges close to me. "Well," she butts in, "we are actually really happy with how well Sarah's doing. This is just some swelling as the fluids flow down from her surgery. She'll look like herself in a few days. You'll see."

The girls engage with Mom, who transfers all the talk to them. How's school? Anyone looking for dresses for the next dance? Who has a date? She spins their enthusiasm away from me until I can get control. I finally give her a little smile, and she nods.

It's Willow who breaks out of Mom's conversation. "But listen to us. This is about you, Sarah." She holds out her hands to me. "Just look at your poor hair! We heard all about it this morning from Luke and Cydni. Your hair won't be back to normal in a few days, will it?"

Kara sets a big bag on the bed. "Which is why we bought you hats!" She pulls them out one by one.

"We got to skip sixth period, and we've been shopping ever since!" squeals Anna.

"And I have to thank you, Sarah!" Laura giggles. "I mean, I got this really cute plaid skirt and tights."

"Oh, great," I manage to say. The berets, sun hats, and baseball caps cover the bed.

Kara grins. "We took a donation today at lunch and then went and bought all of these for you."

I finger one. The girls model them for me. They flip around their hair whenever they take a hat off, checking themselves in the mirror above the flowers and balloons. I can't keep a smile on my face. It keeps sliding off.

"Try this one, Sarah," Anna insists.

"Oh, no. I think, you know, my incision would hurt."

"Oh, sure. I'm sorry."

"Thank you for the gifts, but I think it would be good for Sarah to rest now." Mom walks over to the door.

"Of course, Mrs. McCormick," says Kara. The girls gather in a cluster.

"Thanks for coming," I manage to say.

Kara stops. "Oh, sure. We needed to do a community service project for Pep. So this was, like, perfect!" She leads the way out, everyone following.

My chest is strangled and my face hot.

Mom quips, "It takes everything in me not to kick her tight little butt down the hall."

"Mom!" I surprise us both and laugh.

She raises an eyebrow. "What?"

All the embarrassment I suppressed during their visit suddenly boils up, and I start bawling.

Mom holds on to my trembling knee, crooked beneath the sheet.

"Thanks for helping me out when they were here, Mom, but can you just give me minute alone?" I gasp.

"Sure, honey. I'll go and check on ... um ... something." She disappears into the hall, actually giving me space.

CHAPTER 40

Haddings

Heading into the Starbucks by the hospital, I see them clustered in the middle of the café, laughing and chatting. It's the popular clique from the high school. When I slip into line, I can hear practically every word of their conversation.

Kara sets down her cup and puts her hand to her chest. "I couldn't believe how horrible she looked!"

"Like, what did you think? A frog or a basketball?" says a girl I don't know.

Willow taps her finger into the foam in her cup and daintily dabs it on her tongue. "I just never imagined Sarah would look so bad."

"I know," Laura laughs. "But really, we shouldn't laugh, right?" And then they all do.

Anger curls my fingers. I step out of line and head straight to their group.

"Mr. Haddings!" Kara says, shooting out of her chair.

I slap my palms on the table, rocking their mochas, macchiatos, and fraps. "Don't you ever, ever laugh at Sarah again."

They stare wide-eyed at me, while a few nod quickly.

"No, we didn't mean any — " Kara starts.

"I don't want to hear it." I narrow my eyes and look at them singly. "This was a horrific accident. At least respect that. If you knew any better, you'd respect Sarah."

I walk away from the narcissistic bunch, leaving them speechless for once. Good riddance.

CHAPTER 41

Sarah

Mom, Luke, and Cydni all come back in together. Luke passes me my ice cream without meeting my eyes, but Cydni scoots past him and settles next to me on the bed. I immediately start to recount the Pep Club visit.

"Can you believe that?" I ask.

"Unbelievable," Cydni says.

Dad shows up midway into the story. "Hey, baby," he says.

"Hi, Daddy." I swallow another bite of ice cream.

He looks at Mom strangely, takes her hand, and leads her into the bathroom. "That's weird," I whisper.

Cydni shrugs. "Back to your story." She feeds me a huge spoonful of melty ice cream. "I can't believe they were trying on the hats and everything."

178

"What more can you expect from the most popular girls in the school?" Luke asks. "It's all about looks."

"Right," Cydni agrees, "but real friends won't care what you look like, Sarah. Right, Luke?" Cydni turns to him.

"Yeah," plops out of his mouth, but I know it's not totally true.

While Cydni scrapes the last bite from the cup, Mom and Dad's conversation gets louder and louder through the bathroom door.

When the staff brings in my dinner, I invite Luke and Cydni to share my tater tots while I eat the chicken fingers. We try to cover up my parents' discussion by talking over them, but it's obviously fake, so we peter out and end up listening in.

"Janet, listen."

"What is your point?" Mom complains.

"Let it go, already. Stop wasting energy on those girls. We have nothing to spare right now. Let's focus on taking care of Sarah. Let's take care of you."

"I don't care about me!" Mom says.

"Sooo." Cydni gets up and hands me a napkin. "I'll go get you some more ice for your water pitcher, Sarah. Be right back." She scurries out the door. At least she can escape my parents' fight.

Luke covers his face. "Could they be more embarrassing?"

"Um, no."

Mom keeps it up. "If you'd listen to me, Mark, you'd understand how upset Sarah was."

"I am listening."

"No, like usual, you're standing there in some other place."

"Stop, Janet. Just stop! You don't know how hard I'm trying," Dad says. "Okay. Maybe I haven't always been attentive, but right now, I'm standing here and telling you, you need to let it go! I'm focused this very second, and what I see that matters is you and Sarah. Stop. Look in the mirror. Look, Janet."

I know her hair is ragged; there are bruises below her eyes. She hasn't left here or changed clothes since yesterday before the accident. Luke gets up and paces.

More quietly, Dad says, "Honey, look at your hands. You're shaking from so much caffeine. You need to eat better. Rest. You need to take care of yourself, so you can take care of Sarah."

"No. I don't deserve any attention. You, you don't understand."

"Please, Janet. We all need you. You deserve to take care of yourself and be taken care of," Dad says.

Mom's ragged breath slips under the door. "It's all my—" She sobs out her thoughts. The jumble of sounds heaves out.

Luke and I are completely still until Mom's anguish finally wanes. Somehow she thinks the accident was her fault? "That's crazy," I whisper. Luke shuffles his feet.

"It was an accident, Janet," Dad insists.

Cydni tips her head into the room. Hearing the quiet, she comes in and dumps a cup of ice into my pitcher. She pours me cold water and holds it while I sip from the straw. All's silent behind the bathroom door, and so are we.

When Dad comes out, he rolls the tray with my empty dishes away, and he and Cydni spread my Kentlake blanket across the bed. Our hawk mascot warms me right up. "Thanks for bringing this from home, Dad." I tug it close.

"Sure thing, Sarah." He returns to his book.

Cydni fills me in on the day, how she and Luke were bombarded with questions from all the students and even the teachers. It was hard for the two of them to get through the halls from class to class, so many people were concerned and wanted to hear the latest.

I fill her in on getting out the drainage tube, and decide to skip the catheter and Haddings' visit, let alone how I know he was the driver. Even though she didn't tell me, I don't want to talk about that stuff with Luke here, and I don't need to hear about her disapproval of Haddings when I have enough of my own right now. I'll tell her later.

She putters around the room, straightening, stacking, tidying, but eventually, she sits down next to Luke. Funny how they keep looking at each other. Smiling.

Glancing. Looking.

Smiling again.

Cydni softly giggles at something he says into her ear.

Oh no. Oh, don't even tell me! They are together? No stinking way. Please, please, not that weirdness. My best friend and my brother?

Luke's hand brushes her knee, and she leans closer to him. He doesn't pull back, and knocks his shoulder against hers.

I purse my lips and stare up at the IV, the droplets going down into the tube. So, what, guys? This all happened while I lay here bloated? Or when I was in surgery? When they were cutting open my head? Or drilling my skull back together? How insensitive can you be?

I sniffle, and no one notices. I can't believe it. I kick at my sheets. They don't look over.

Great. Just great. The bottom line is that my best friend gets my brother while I don't get Haddings. Jealousy gurgles my guts, burning up into my throat. I swallow it down along with the tantrum that wants to blast out of me at them.

After a few minutes, I make myself look again. Cydni smiles at Luke. Dad's oblivious, reading.

I count the holes in the ceiling tiles.

Cydni giggles again. She's definitely happy. I close my eyes, trying to chill. "Luke," she flirts. I go to glare at them but see reality; for once, she's really happy. Luke sets his hand on her arm.

I pick at the tape on my own hand. Oh, come on. Like I wouldn't have done the same if it had been Haddings or someone like him? If Luke or Cydni were in a life or death situation, and there was a super long wait, and the guy was perfect? Not that Luke is, but Cydni thinks so.

No, I still wouldn't move that fast. Luke shares a mint with her and clicks the tin closed.

They have known each other for forever though. Did he lean on her through this whole thing or something? Cydni would have swooned over that. She can at least thank me for the opportunity later. Sheesh.

Luke's eyes slide from Cydni. Remarkably, he looks at me for a sec. I bury my jealousy for now, somehow, and shrug toward her. He grins. "Thanks," he mouths.

I scooch up in bed a smidge, a tiny bit stronger. What a total surprise.

6:23 pm

When Mom comes out of the bathroom, she's in clean clothes. Her hair's brushed smooth with her bangs swept to the side. Her eyes are red from crying, but her brow isn't squeezed like it has been. She sits in a chair while Dad stands behind her and rubs her shoulders.

"Dinner was good, Mom. I ate a lot."

"That's nice, dear." Now her lips turn up into a little smile, and she closes her eyes. There's no doubt my mom is beautiful. Everyone always says I look like her.

What about now? I bite my lip. Seems I should know how I look, right? Everyone else has seen. Even Haddings.

An urgency zooms through me. I need to see. Right now. I need to see what I look like. Maybe, maybe it isn't so bad.

"I want to — " Everyone turns to me, including Haddings in the doorway.

"I have to apologize to everyone, Sarah," he says.

"Can I help you?" Mom asks.

"Is there something — " Dad says.

"Mr. Haddings!" Cydni yelps.

Luke launches across the room, the power pumping off him. He coils his arm back and lets it fly. His fist connects with Haddings' eye, and Haddings stumbles out into the hallway.

Everyone is yelling at Luke. Where's the hospital staff? Isn't anyone hearing this?

Luke lunges for Haddings, grabs his arm, and yanks him back into my room. "Do you see what you did to my sister? Do you?" He spits the words out. Punches him again.

"Luke!" Mom yells.

Dad grabs Luke's arms and wrestles him off Haddings.

"Look at her!" Luke shouts and kicks out. "Look at what you did!"

Haddings takes it all. Doesn't defend himself.

Where did all that come from, Luke? I quickly remember to close my mouth, suppress my grin. My chest warms with the light my brother just ignited inside of me.

"It was Haddings who hit you," Cydni whispers to me.

"I know," I smile at her.

CHAPTER 42

Haddings

6:27 pm

He connected well. My eye is already swelling; there's blood on
my lip, but I stand there, with my arms hanging at my sides,
waiting for the next hit. Someone, hurt me worse than I hurt
Sarah. Please.

"Is everything all right?" a nurse asks at the door.

"Yes," they answer.

I don't turn around. She pauses, then leaves.

CHAPTER 43

Sarah

Luke wipes his tears on his shoulder. He wrenches himself free of Dad and goes to stand beside Cydni. She squeezes his forearm. "You were awesome!" she says.

Mom's in the corner of the room, looking remarkably small. Dad blocks Haddings from Luke with his body, but all of a sudden something goes off in him. His fists close, and in two steps he's thrown Haddings up against the wall.

"Do you see my daughter?" he mutters. "I could kill you."

As we all gasp, Haddings looks him straight in the eye.

Dad rattles him against the wall. "That's my daughter! You hit her, and now you want me to hit you, don't you? To punish you. Well, forget it." He shoves Haddings aside. "I won't give you the relief."

185

Mom pulls Dad to her.

"After all my talk, this blasts out of me?" he asks her, then turns to me. "I'm sorry, honey, but I honestly could pummel him to death."

My eyes widen, and I hurry to say, "It's okay, Daddy. Thanks for defending me."

He gently sweeps the tears off my cheek.

I snivel, and the light I got from Luke spreads brighter through my whole body, even in and around my cracked skull. My outrage, my anger, dims.

"I guess everyone knows, this is Mr. Haddings," I say. He stares at me with so much sorrow I almost feel bad for him.

He steps to the center of the room and looks at each of them. "I am so sorry," he repeats to each person. "I don't expect your forgiveness, but I do want you to know, I am sorry, and we'll cover all the costs. My family and I."

No one will look at him, except me. After catching my eye, he loses it in front of everyone.

Heartless, Mom just shakes her head and crosses her arms, while Dad squeezes the bridge of his nose. Luke rubs his fist, and Cydni glares at the floor.

"Um. Can everyone, like, go get something to eat or something?" I say.

Haddings moves to leave.

"Not you," I say. "Everyone else."

"Is it safe?" Mom asks.

"No way," says Luke. "No way can we leave her here alone with this guy. Are you kidding me?"

Ignoring Cydni, who is beaming death rays at Haddings, I plead with Dad until he caves. "Please?"

"Well, it's not my choice, but I think it will be okay. It's not as if he's going to run her over with her table tray."

I shake my head. "Dad."

No one moves for a second. And then several more.

Finally Dad takes a big breath, and it whistles out of him again. "Come on, Luke. Cydni. Janet. You sure, baby girl? This is what you really want?"

I pull up my sheet. "Uh huh. I need this. Please, Dad? Just a few minutes."

He nods to the door, and, miraculously, they all follow him out of the room. Even my mom goes, although she looks at me, a question on her face. If she suspects anything, she doesn't say so and leaves. The whispers and footsteps start and stop but eventually diminish.

It's just me and Haddings.

CHAPTER 44

Haddings

Sarah looks up at me. "Is your eye okay?"

"Doesn't matter." I blot my face on my sleeve.

"Here." She presses one of her cold packs into my hand. "Put that on your eye."

I shake my head. The ice clinks in the quiet.

Finally, Sarah speaks up. "I told you, you should wait to come back."

"No, it was right to face them."

"It wouldn't have been so bad if you had waited. They would have had time to cool off," she says.

I shrug.

She shakes her head. "Well, since you're here, maybe you could help me."

"Anything," I answer.

"I didn't want everyone here, but I don't want to be alone, either. I need to look in the mirror — if you could stay with me for a minute."

I startle at her words. "Really?" I ask. "You sure you don't want me to call your mom back?"

She rolls her lips inward. "No."

CHAPTER 45

Sarah

6:35 pm

"I have to see sometime. There's going to be a mirror somewhere, and I'd rather look on purpose than be caught by surprise."

"Sounds smart," he agrees. "And, it's the least I can do." He sets the cold pack down on my tray.

"Yeah." A little payback. "Would you shut the door, if you don't mind being alone for a minute?"

"It seems okay, this one time; don't you think?" Closing the door, he smiles sadly, then walks over and moves the flower bouquets aside. "Ready?"

"Yes."

He parts the balloons, and I press the button, tilting the bed up higher, and look into the mirror. My nightmare.

"Uhhhhhhh!" I can't move, blink, or speak. I stare, until

the shock lets go of its hold. I pull my pillow to my mouth and wail. From the bottom of my belly, I cry, filling the room with my muted horror.

Who am I without half of my hair, with a mangled, puffed face? Groans glump out of me. I claw my blanket. "I'm horribly ugly!" And all these people have been looking at me? How can they stand it? Stand it enough to help me? How in the world can they still love me? "I'm so ugly!"

"No, no, Sarah," Haddings argues.

"Why? Why did you hit me with your car? Why, Haddings?" I rock and sob.

Looking at me through the mirror, he cries silently.

Reality slips. I raise my hands to claw at my head. I want the stitches out! Right now.

Haddings lets go of the balloons, which bob over to the window. He jumps to my side. Clamping my wrists, he holds my arms down beside my hip. I writhe and buck against him.

"Stop, Sarah," he pleads. "Stop it!"

My agony bursts from my soul in gapping breaths.

"Oh, Sarah!" His tears drip onto the sheet. "I'm so sorry!"

I can't. I can't fight him. I give one last jolt and collapse, gasping, riding the pain.

My head threatens to pop at the seam. I rock the pain, rock it until the beat slows. The pulsing waves crash, curl smaller to a seven on the pain scale. My body jerks on its own.

Haddings finally loosens his grip but stays beside me. When I look again, the mirror shows my fat face, smeared with ointment, tears, and snot.

Despite the extra pain, I roll into the pillowcase and curl into a circle on my side. "I'm hideous."

191

His soft words slide over my shoulder and fall into my ear. "No, I am."

6:46 pm

I eventually sit quietly and stare at myself in the mirror. Haddings wets the washcloth and tenderly blots my face, dabbing the blood seeping from the incision. He pulls my blanket straight.

"How can you look at me?" I ask.

He dries my eyes. "It's only hard knowing I'm the one who made you look this way."

When he perches beside me on the bed, I rest my ear gently against his arm. We sit silently while I examine every inch of my face. Only our jerky breath from crying breaks the quiet.

The noise of their fight tumbles down the hallway into our silence. Haddings jumps off the bed and opens the door. Their voices grow louder. "We all know it's his fault, Dad, but what about me?" Luke asks. "I should have given her a ride. If I had hurried, she wouldn't have been crossing the street and been hit! It's my fault she looks like this!"

My dad cuts him off. "No! I could have driven her! If I had focused on her instead of on my own breakfast."

Mom starts in. "No! I'm her mother! It's my responsibility to protect Sarah."

And finally Cydni's voice spins above everyone's. "Why wasn't it me who got hit?"

A nurse routes them all into my room. She tugs her printed cap straight. "Please, please!" she says with a Jamaican accent, "you are disturbing the other patients. Sarah, are you all right? Do you need everyone to leave?"

"I'm fine," I insist.

The nurse puts her fists on her hips. "You've all been warned." She gives them the evil eye and turns on her heel. "Warned, mind you," she says over her shoulder.

Mom notices the uncovered mirror. "Sarah?"

"It's okay." I rub my palms on my blanket. "You can all stop pretending. I know how horrific I look." I let out a puff of air. "Worse than Luke said."

"Sarah, no—"

I interrupt my mom. "I saw. Stop already." She rolls her lips. I take a giant, cleansing breath. "And you all can stop the drama." I slowly lift my eyes to Haddings. "It was just an accident."

At once, they apologize on top of each other. "I'm so sorry, honey," says Mom.

Cydni apologizes. "I'm sorry."

"Sorry, baby girl," Dad adds.

"Sorry, Sares," says Luke.

Haddings finishes it off. "No, I'm sorry, everyone."

Dottie sticks her head into the room. "There you are, beautiful! I wanted to stop on in before my shift starts and check on you."

"Hi," I say.

Haddings blows his nose and wipes his face.

"It looks like you could use some ice." Dottie pulls a fresh cold pack from a tray in the hall and hands it to Haddings. "Put it on your eye now." He does. "Hey," she greets everyone lined up against the wall like they are facing a firing squad.

"Hey," they collectively repeat.

Did Dottie hear them yelling at each other? Or me freaking earlier with Haddings? Wait. Did she call me beautiful?

"Now look'a there," she says, filling my cup with water. "Those fluids from your surgery are coming down wonderfully." I pull in a long drink through the straw, and then Dottie sets the cup on my tray. "Boy, it does my heart good to see you healing so quickly. You definitely are on the mend, young lady. Mm-hmm. Just a little bleeding there, I see."

She tugs the washcloth from Haddings' fist and drops it in the laundry bin. With gauze, Dottie dabs the heat from my face. "There you go." She rinses a fresh cloth and drapes it on my neck. Crossing her arms over her broad belly, she says, "Pretty as a picture, Sarah. Y'all know, they say after it's been shaved, hair grows in thicker than before. Don't 'cha?"

"I've heard," I manage to answer. "But I can see the mirror, so I know what I look like, Dottie."

She holds my gaze. "What I see is your spirit, young lady. Listen here." She ticks off the points on her thick fingers. "It's not full of self-pity. It's not brewing anger over how this all happened. It may be mourning, but that's healthy. It's trying to rest, making sure you eat, and loving these people gathered around you." She takes my finger and checks my oxygen. "You can't imagine what I most often see in tragedies like these. You are showing a large measure of grace, m'dear."

I blush. Mom and Dottie meant on the inside. I have felt ugly there, too, but listening to her, I can see there is a measure of grace I didn't notice. Grace I never even thought to be thankful for. Just the fact I can be around Haddings is something, right?

Dottie grins at my family and friends. "Isn't it nice to have such kind people around you who absolutely love each other and you?"

Haddings catches my eye.

194

Dottie goes on. "Mm hmm. It truly makes all the difference in a recovery."

Mom picks her chipped nail polish. Dad rubs his nose. Luke cracks his knuckles. Cydni redoes her pony knot, and Haddings is looking at Dottie like she has every answer there is.

She flips through my chart. "And look'a there. You are going home sooner than expected! Blessings are always tucked inside difficulties."

"What?" I ask.

"Oh, certainly." She pries the blanket from my grip. One big flap and the Kentlake hawk floats gently down over me. "It's like that tough, leathery pomegranate I bought yesterday," she says. "Inside, it was full of glistening, sweet red seeds. Well, then." She rocks in her orange clogs. "I need to skedaddle. Just wanted to stop in and wish you well. You take good care of each other now."

I smile. Mom and Dad manage a thanks and good-bye, then Dottie's out the door.

Seeds. I'm surrounded by people who love me even when I look like this and am such a burden, needing their help for everything. My skin tingles.

Dad pats my foot. Tucking her hair behind her ear, Mom says, "I'm so sorry I can't keep bad things from happening to you, Sarah."

I squeeze her hand. "I get that."

Cydni nudges Luke, who says, "Yeah. I wanted to say, to tell you, if you come back to school, I'll be with you. Even if you look like this. I mean, if, you know, you wear a hat."

"Luke!" Cydni shakes his arm, but I laugh, and my parents groan.

195

Cydni sits on the stool beside me. "Sarah, I do wonder why it wasn't me that got hit, but you are dealing with everything better than I ever could. The helicopter, the pain, you know what I'm saying? You are amazing. I mean, how can you even stand to have him" — she tilts her head at Haddings — "near you. That's incredible."

I look down and fiddle with my IV tape. "Thanks?"

Haddings moves to the corner of the room, beside the roses. Everyone else snugs close to my bed.

"I'm fine with taking the bus, you know. I wanted to take the bus."

"We know," say Mom and Dad.

"I guess," Luke mumbles, then looks at me straight on. He holds my gaze, and his energy shoots into my veins. "We just want you to know, we care about you and stuff."

"I know that," I whisper and pet my blanket so all the furries lie flat on the hawk's back. "It doesn't hurt to hear you feel bad for me though."

Haddings covers his face.

"Everyone can use a little sympathy," says Mom.

"I guess."

Cydni looks to my father. "Why do you think this happened? Like, why did Sarah get hit?"

Dad massages his neck and sits on my bed. "I don't know why," he admits. Mom places her palm on Dad's back, and he sits up straighter. "I can't presume that I'll ever understand, but I do know there will be good in it for Sarah."

Dad's surety seeps into me.

Luke rolls his eyes. "That is so unbelievable."

"Yeah, I'm sorry, Mr. McCormick, but that reeks." Cydni

196

shakes her head, making her hair knot wobble on the top of her head. "I don't see any good."

Dad sighs. "Ultimately, everything is a test of faith, Cydni, and that's the solace."

Mom nods once; Luke shakes his head, no; Cydni looks away, but I catch Dad's eye.

That's the solace.

CHAPTER 46

Haddings

That is heavy. Too heavy. The whys and what fors. All I can deal with is that I was the one driving the car. I hit Sarah; now, what can I do? A sigh pops from my lips, and they turn to me.

"I want to say again that I'm here for Sarah, whatever she needs."

I stare at this girl, who I knew was amazing before, and see an intensity beyond what I imagined. "I'm not going to disappear." I straighten my shirt then drop my hands. "I won't walk away if … you don't keep me away."

CHAPTER 47

Sarah

He looks at me like that when I look like this? It's not like he's family and has to be here. He's always saying I'm his responsibility because he's my teacher and I'm his student. But really, there's no responsibility, beyond finances with him being the driver. Is it only guilt making him say all that?

I finger the gross ends of my hair. How can he relate to me even better than before, when I wasn't stitched, shaved, and swollen? How? Can he see inside me, too? My lip quivers and my wonderment feels fatter than my face.

"You believe me, right? That I'll be here through everything?" Haddings asks my parents.

With crossed arms, my mom shrugs while my dad bites the

inside corner of his mouth. "We'll see," he says. Mom picks up my paperwork and points out something to Dad.

Cydni walks close and stands by Haddings. "I'm not sorry that I said those things at the bus stop to you."

What in the world did she say?

He looks straight at her. "I deserve worse."

Agreement skitters over everyone's faces.

When Haddings excuses himself for a few minutes to make a couple calls, I watch him leave, a little smile on my face.

Luke catches my eye. He raises his left brow.

"What?" I mouth.

"Are you serious?" he whispers over Cydni's shoulder as she moves my magazines to make room to sit next to him.

I glance at Mom and Dad, but they are still reviewing the pile of paperwork.

"Sarah," Luke hisses. "No!"

How did he see into my heart, maybe before I even could?

Cydni sits down beside Luke and leans against his shoulder. She slips her hand into his, and Luke starts to calm down. She gives me a sly smile, which I make myself return. No worries, I brainwave to her. She blushes. Finally, she has what she wants, even if I don't. For her, I know I can get over it. Soon enough.

Luke gets up and comes close. "Please, I need some time to figure everything out," I whisper to him. "There's nothing going on, but maybe someday, you know?"

He tilts his head. "All right." I smile the biggest since surgery. "But if he hurts you again," he whispers back, "even a speck, there's his other eye. Plus, I drive a truck."

I lean my cheek against his chest, and he doesn't pull away.

Mom and Dad are called to the nurses' station to discuss home care and next steps for my release. When Haddings comes back, Luke and Cydni admit they should head out to do their homework.

Luke takes one more long look at Haddings though. "I can't say I'm really sorry about, you know ..."

Haddings touches his eye and flinches. "Understood."

"I'll be watching you," my brother postures.

"Okay, Luke." I laugh.

"No, he has every right," Haddings says.

"You know it." Cydni pushes past him. "Bye." She gives me a kiss on the cheek, and then they are gone, hand in hand, which still twists my heart because I've lost that with Haddings. Or at least the possibility. Even though he's my little brother, Cydni will feel cherished. She better, or I'll be all over Luke like he was on Haddings. Period.

As soon as they leave, Haddings reaches out and covers my hand with his. "I'm serious when I said I'll be here for you. If that's okay?"

A thousand thoughts flood my brain. University of Washington. Mills College. Guilt versus attraction. Duty versus love. Friendship with Haddings or being alone, at least for the foreseeable future. School versus guy relationships. Forgiveness versus anger. Me versus us, when there never really was an "us," although I won't give up that I caught his eye. Finding out who I am now versus trying to return to who I was. Good versus bad. Right versus wrong. Ultimately, what's best for me solely.

I grab onto what my head knows, backed by my gut, and hold

it tightly before it slips away. "That's really sweet, but I don't want you to feel like — actually, I don't need — " He doesn't move away. "I'll be fine. I mean, I don't know what kind of therapy is coming, or how my brain is going to work. Hopefully, it's the same. It seems like it will be once I get all the drugs out of my system." Pause for a giant breath. "But I really think I've decided I'm going to be working my hardest to get to Mills. To take that scholarship. It's really clear now that I have to choose the best for my future. I have to choose for me."

"Mills?" he asks.

"Yeah," I say. "Creative writing and book art. It's what I first wanted, and I realize it still is."

He holds his chin. "You'll be at Mills."

"I hope so."

CHAPTER 48

Haddings

If all is well with her mind, I'm going to lose her to Mills. She's not going to UW, where I would have the chance to be with her. Of course not, after what I've done. It's not the choice she should have considered to begin with.

I teeter on the edge of her bed and pull her journal from my pocket. The tiniest smile flickers over her swollen lips. I open the book and add a poem as she watches. I found it in a collection earlier today when I was hanging in Elliot Bay Book Company. I couldn't shake it while I wandered through Pike Place Market. It made me come back tonight. It's the truth, and I have to let her know.

La Vita Nuova

In that book which is
My memory ...
On the first page
That is the chapter when
I first met you
Appear the words ...
Here begins a new life

Dante Alighieri

Sarah's hand hovers over the words like she's calling them off the page. "I'll be here, Sarah. Right here," I say.

She's silent a moment and then says, "And hopefully, I'll be at Mills."

CHAPTER 49

Sarah

He touches the back of my hand, like a breeze caressing a rose, but jerks away frightened when he brushes against my IV. "I'm sorry!" he blurts.

"No, it's fine," I say, "but you have been saying that a lot lately."

"I'm a fool," he whispers.

"Yeah," I whisper back, but before he can step away, I reach out and open his fisted hand pressed to his heart. I set my fingers on his trembling ones. "It's okay," I say. "It's okay."

CHAPTER 50

Haddings

I slide into my car and adjust the rearview mirror. Talking out my plans, I clarify everything. "I'll close out this semester. After that, my master's is on hold until I can take care of whatever debt accrues from the accident. My parents won't mortgage their home. I'll go full-time waiting tables and find a roommate or two to cut housing costs. It's possible I could trade in my Mustang for something cheaper."

I turn the key in the ignition, and the car purrs around me. "If there's a civil suit, I'll work longer." I buckle my seat belt. "This is right. This is my truth. It's not grand plans that matter; it's the small things I will do to make this right: paying the bills, protecting you from ridiculous peers, and offering any kind of tutoring you might need." I back up out of the parking space and drive from the garage.

"You are worth it, Sarah. Just watch me show you."

CHAPTER 51

Sarah

8:52 pm

With Luke, Cydni, and Haddings gone and the nurses giving me a break, my folks fall asleep leaning against each other in front of the TV. I hit the mute button and gaze out the window, beyond our reflection. Stars and city lights dot the night settled on Seattle.

I click off the TV, and my eyes slowly adjust in the darkness. I inhale at the sight out the window now. The deep blue silhouette of Mt. Rainier rises on the horizon, immense and beautiful, reflecting light I can't even see.

Emily Dickinson was right.

> "Hope" is the thing with feathers —
> That perches in the soul —

And sings the tune without the words —
And never stops — at all —

I click on the little bed light and pick up my poetry journal.
After rereading Haddings' poem, I turn to a fresh, clean page.
Flying on the flutters of hope, I write:

I hope
I can totally forgive one day,
nothing held back
or buried out of sight;
I hope
I will heal completely, mind
and body;
I hope
I can love my family
the way they show love to me;
I hope
maybe he will be waiting,
if, and only if,
that's what
I truly want.

PART 3

Day Three

CHAPTER 52

Sarah

8:30 am

The nurse, Kate, wheels me out of the hospital into the fresh air. In only three days, they let me go.

"It's too soon," Luke said.

"Modern medicine," Dad countered.

"Less chance of infection," Mom added.

I only want to get home. The rain pops in the puddles around our car. I pull my hood closer to my face.

At the curb, Kate puts on the wheelchair brake. I smile at the Super Grovers printed all over her scrubs. "This is a new beginning. Stay positive, Sarah."

"I'm trying," I say. "Could you help me, Mom?"

"Happy to." She smiles and takes my arm. Luke takes my other one. I nose my toes down into the scary crosswalk. My legs wiggle. My ankles give out, but Cydni pulls me into the car. "Come on, bestie," she says, and Luke lifts my feet inside.

I curl up in the moment until the shakes still. Mom reaches in and squeezes my shoulder. "You're okay," she says. "You're doing great!"

Dad winks at me through the rearview mirror.

I inch over and catch my massive green face in the reflection. Sheesh. I look like Shrek. But I'm still me inside. I take another look. Yep. That's me, no matter how hideous, or confused, or slow. Loved and loving.

The car rocks as Mom and Luke climb in. Luke squishes me up against Cydni. "Oof," she says. I laugh at the normality, even though it hurts.

I do a measly shove back against my brother. "Be careful," I say.

"Mom," Luke whines. "Sarah's on my side."

Mom shakes her head, but she smiles wryly. "Hey, I like that hoodie on you, Sarah."

I grin. "Thanks. Bought it myself."

"What a perfect choice," she adds.

"Onward!" says Dad.

Cydni reaches over and holds my hand. I lean forward and lift my face in the sun shaft slipping through the window.

A poem Haddings read in class flits into my mind. The one by Raymond Carver, and I feel joy. Really feel it.

Late Fragment

And did you get what
you wanted from this life, even so?
I did.

And what did you want?
To call myself beloved, to feel myself
beloved on earth.